D0575286

MUSIC
for children

MUSIC
for children

Rebecca Rumens-Syratt

BATSFORD

First published in the United Kingdom in 2016 by
Batsford
1 Gower Street
London WC1E 6HD

An imprint of Pavilion Books Company Ltd

ISBN: 9781849943093

A CIP catalogue record for this book is available from the British Library.

10 9 8 7 6 5 4 3 2 1

Reproduction by Colourdepth UK
Printed and bound by Toppan Leefung, China

This book can be ordered direct from the publisher at the website:
www.pavilionbooks.com, or try your local bookshop.

Contents

1
READING MUSIC

Reading music is a very useful skill for any musician. Symbols and lines and dots all come together when we know how to interpret them and we can turn them into beautiful sounds on the spot. Also, if you can read music you can learn how to write music so you can capture your tunes and ideas forever and pass them on to other people to play! When you were younger you learnt to read letters and words and it was hard at first, but here you are, reading this book! With practice we can learn to understand our musical 'words' and 'sentences' too.

Music as a language

Music is great! Wherever we are in the world, we will have heard some sort of music and many of us have sung along with a favourite song or tapped out a **rhythm** with our hands and feet. People sometimes call music a 'universal language', because even people who don't speak the same language can make music together.

However old you are, you can enjoy music by listening to it, singing, or playing an instrument. Playing instruments together in a group helps us to make friends and teaches us about working with other people. As well as being fun, playing and singing exercises our muscles and our brain.

Learning music can help us in lots of other areas, too. It makes us better at reading and writing, because we learn music through reading its symbols. We have to count the **beats** and rhythms in music, and this helps us with mental maths. The way sound is made and heard is all to do with air vibrations and waves: we are studying science without even realizing it. If we start performing music to an audience, it helps us become more confident in everyday life.

Trudi Treble

Hi! My name is Trudi Treble. People often use me as a symbol for all music. You'll learn more about me in Chapter 2. I like all types of music, but what is your favourite? Can you name any musicians?

Italian words

Italian words are used to describe the way music should be played. Use an app or the Internet to find the meaning of these Italian words:

lento

vivace

forte

rallentando

canto

Can you find any more?

So how do we start to learn about music? Music has its own special words to describe musical things. But don't worry: we'll be explaining these as we go, and you can also look them up in the glossary. Musicians will often say things that don't make sense to other people such as, 'Let's take it from the head!' They're not talking about real heads! They mean the beginning of the main tune or chorus of a song.

As well as words, musical symbols tell musicians what to do. Music is written down using signs and symbols – just like letters and lines make sentences and paragraphs. Some symbols are called **notes**. Each note stands for a different sound. Other symbols explain how to play the notes. Most musicians learn how to read music symbols, so when someone gives them a new song they can play it straight away! We call the skill of looking at music symbols and being able to create the sounds they stand for **'sight-reading'**.

Come with us on a musical journey: learn the language of music and you can become a great sight-reader!

Barry Bass

The stave

When we look at a sheet of music, the symbols and notes are written on a **stave**. The stave is a set of five lines for placing musical ideas on. We can follow these lines like a train track, from the beginning of the music piece to the end. The stave is split up into even sections called **bars**, which act as signposts to where we are in the music, like signal posts along a train track. We will learn more about bars later.

Did you know?

You can buy books ruled with music staves, instead of lines, to write music on. We call this **manuscript paper**. Find it in a stationery shop and buy some to practise writing music on.

Time to introduce you to my best friend, Barry Bass!

Clefs

Trudi Treble and Barry Bass are the squiggly musical symbols called **clefs**. A clef tells us how high or low the music is going to sound. It appears on the stave.

In music we use a series of words to describe whether things sound high or low:

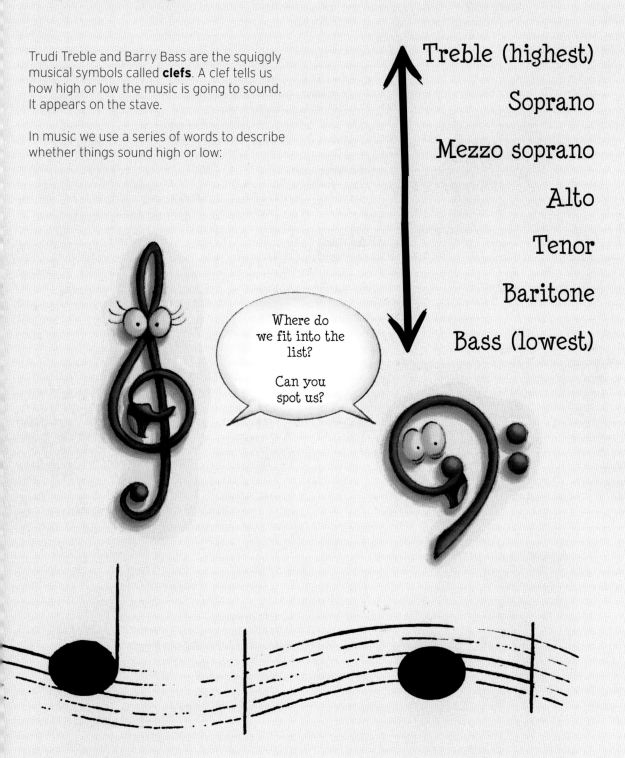

Treble (highest)

Soprano

Mezzo soprano

Alto

Tenor

Baritone

Bass (lowest)

Where do we fit into the list?

Can you spot us?

In earlier times, people used a different clef for every one of these words, but that was confusing. Now we mainly use two - treble and bass (like Trudi and Barry!) - for high and low. Music for some instruments still uses the alto clef or tenor clef.

Alisha Alto

Tom Tenor

Hi! We're Alisha Alto and Tom Tenor. We look the same, but sound different. Remember us, because we'll be popping back later to tell you about some special instruments that read music off us.

All notes are named after letters in the alphabet: A, B, C, D, E, F, G. One very special note is called **middle C**. It is roughly in the middle of a piano's keyboard and is easy for most people to sing and for most instruments to play. We will learn about other notes later.

Middle C sounds exactly the same whichever clef it is in. It sounds the same but looks different on the stave for each clef. This also means we sometimes call the alto and tenor clefs the C clefs.

In the treble clef, middle C sits on its own little line below the stave. In the bass clef, it sits on its own little line above the stave. On a printed sheet of music, the treble clef is placed above the bass clef. As middle C is the same sound in both clefs, we can imagine that the middle C line is an extra train track running alongside the bass and treble clefs, and this is where the notes cross over.

Some instruments have a really wide **range**, which means that they can play many notes between their highest note and their lowest note. A piano is a good example. Music for the piano is written in both bass clef and treble clef. To play it, you read music off the two lines together. Mostly, the bass clef bits are played with the left hand, at the low end of the piano, and the high notes in the treble clef are played with the right hand.

Middle C

Make edible music!

You will need:
- A clean dinner tray
- Strawberry liquorice laces
- Small, round sweets

This is a great (and tasty) way to make music at home. Pull out five long strawberry laces and place them on the tray in evenly spaced lines. These are the stave. Take a small handful of round sweets for making the notes and shake them lightly over the laces. Make a sketch or take a picture of where they fall. Which notes have you made? Work it out by looking at the rhymes on the next page.

Some **composers** (people who write new music) actually come up with their ideas in this way! Other ways include rolling dice or flipping a coin. You can eat your music now ...

Notes

Now we know that the stave holds the notes of music, we need to know how to read them. Some notes sit on the lines of the stave; other notes sit between the lines. Look at the pictures below. We are now going to give each finger and space a letter to represent a note and make up some rhymes to help us remember them.

Bass notes

Let's start with the bass clef. (Remember Barry Bass?) The left hand is going to show the notes in the bass clef, starting with the little finger and working towards the thumb. The notes that sit on the lines of the stave are G, B, D, F, A. Remember them like this:

Green

Buses

Drive

Fast

Always

The notes that sit between the lines of the stave are A, C, E, G. Starting with the space between little finger and fourth finger, we can remember those notes with the rhyme:

All

Cows

Eat

Grass

Notice that in music, it is very important to always count up from the bottom or lowest note.

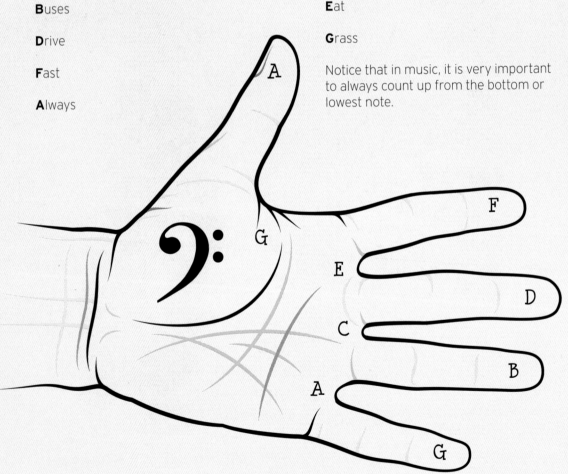

Treble notes

Now let's learn the notes in the treble clef. We'll use our right hand, working from little finger to thumb. The notes that sit on the lines of the stave are E, G, B, D, F. Remember them like this:

Every

Good

Boy

Deserves

Football

The notes that sit between the lines of the stave are F, A, C, E. Starting with the space between the little finger and fourth finger, we can remember those notes with a simple word: 'face'.

Word music

Can you work out the secret messages hidden in these musical notes? Use the rhymes to work out the letters of each note and write them down to spell out a word. Can you make any note words of your own?

Pitch and melody

The higher a note is on the lines of the stave, the higher it sounds. Remember, the treble clef sounds higher than the bass clef. Highs and lows in music are called **pitch**.

We can stick notes of different pitches together to make a tune or a **melody**. However, we have to choose notes carefully or the music will sound strange (unless, of course, that is the effect we're after!). A melody comes from steps or leaps between notes.

Steps make nice tunes, but these can get a bit boring. Leaps up and down make a melody more interesting. Small leaps are better for a tune, such as a jump of three, four or five notes. Leaps of over five notes can sound sudden and bumpy, and are harder to sing or play. The way we choose which notes to use depends on which **key** our melody is in.

Steps and half-steps

In music, the distance between any two notes - the difference in sound - is called an interval. Intervals are made up of steps and half-steps. A half-step is the same as a note called a semitone.

The difference between a C and a D is 2 steps or counts through the pattern of notes or letters of the alphabet. We call the number of steps between notes an interval, like a gap. The step of 2 between C and D is then called an interval of a 2nd. The difference between a C and a G is five steps: C, D, E, F and G. so we call this an interval of a 5th. Remember we include the start note when counting! If you look at the piano diagram on the next page, you will see there are black notes between the C & D, D & E, F & G, G & A and A & B; we will learn more about these soon. However, there are no black notes between the E & F and the B & C. These are still 2 steps when we count the notes e.g. B-C, but because there is no note in-between, the gap is smaller. This is a half-step or a semitone. The gap between the C and D, because there is a black note in-between, is a whole step or a tone. Both a tone and a semitone are an interval of a 2nd, just different types.

Scales

When we put together a row of notes that move by steps, we call it a **scale**. A scale starts and finishes on the same note (but higher or lower), and has a regular pattern of steps in-between, depending on what sort of scale it is. This is a C scale:

C D E F G A B C

Remember that we only use the letters A-G in music notes. All scales have seven different notes, starting from the **keynote** or **tonic** of the scale, in this case, the letter C. After that, they start repeating themselves, just higher or lower. So, when we get to G, we start again with A.

We can give each step of the scale a different colour to show which number of the scale it is: we call this '**degrees of the scale**'. So C is the tonic, or 1st degree, represented by the colour red in the diagrams below; D is the 2nd degree and is represented by orange, and so on. Every time we repeat a musical letter, it sounds the same but higher or lower. So, in the C scale we have a low C at the beginning and a high C at the end. We call this gap of eight notes an **octave**.

Let's have a look at our C scale on the piano.

Sharps and flats

Can you see that the black keys lie between some of our letter notes? These black keys are where notes called **flats** and **sharps** live. We can vary the pitch of a note by adding a flat or a sharp. A note's sharp is the black key to its right; it makes the note a semitone or half-step higher. A note's flat is the black key to its left; it makes the note a semitone or half-step lower.

To write a flat note, we use a symbol that looks like a squashed 'b'. It is added to a note's letter. A sharp has a symbol similar to a hashtag, and this too is added to the note's letter. So the letter names of the notes are like this:

There are five sharps in an octave: C♯, D♯, F♯, G♯ and A♯. There are also five flats: D♭, E♭, G♭, A♭ and B♭. Notice that each sharp has a matching flat, so for example C♯ and D♭ are the same note!

Major and minor scales

Look at the C scale. It has a specific pattern of steps, which are just white keys, so we call it a **major scale**. If we played every single note between C and the next C (including the black keys), that would also be a scale, but a different kind, called a **chromatic scale**.

What happens if we actually start a scale on an A? We get a scale that goes:

A B C D E F G A

A becomes the tonic, or 1st degree note, and B becomes the 2nd degree note. C is now the 3rd degree, and so on. However, it has a different pattern of steps to the C major scale, and if you listen to it, it sounds quite different, too. We call this pattern of steps a minor scale.

If you can, have a go at playing these scales on a piano or keyboard. What does the major scale sound like? What does the minor scale sound like? How would you describe them?

Hi Trudi. Many people say that major scales sound happy and minor scales sound sad. What do you think?

Yes I agree, Barry, but the chromatic scale sounds quite different, doesn't it? What sort of mood do you think the chromatic scale makes?

You can find out more about playing the piano on page 101

We could also play a major scale starting on a D. However, to keep the same pattern of steps in the scale and make it sound the same as the C major scale, we would have to use some of those sharps and flats on the black keys. The D major scale has an F♯ and a C♯ in it like this:

We can also make a D minor scale. To make the pattern of steps needed for a minor scale, we lose the sharps again and add in a B♭.

Key

Melodies can be based on any of the scales, and some composers choose their favourite or one they feel has a particular mood. The composer needs to tell us which sharps or flats to play throughout the melody, and so writes them at the beginning of the music like this:

This is called the **key signature**. Musicians learn all the scales and the number of sharps and flats they have, so they can tell which key to play in just by looking at the key signature.

The number of sharps and flats changes between all the keys, major and minor. However, the order in which they happen never changes. We know the scale of D major has two sharps – F♯ and C♯. F♯ is the most common sharp. Remember the scale of D minor? It has one flat – B♭, the most common flat.

Order of sharps

If a key is sharp, the sharps will appear in a certain order. The order of sharps is: F♯, C♯, G♯, D♯, A♯, E♯, B♯. We can use a rhyme to help us remember it:

Father **C**hristmas **G**ave **D**ad **A**n **E**lectric **B**lanket

If a key has one sharp, it is the first one in the list. If a key has two sharps, these are the first two on the list, and so on. So, for a key that has four sharps in it, we count through the rhyme, starting from F♯:

F♯ C♯ G♯ D♯

This key signature is E major.

Order of flats

If a key is flat, the flats will appear in a certain order. The order of flats is B♭, E♭, A♭, D♭, G♭, C♭, F♭. The rhyme we can use to help us remember it is:

Blanket **E**xplodes **A**nd **D**ad **G**ets **C**old **F**eet

Notice how the order of flats is the same as the order of sharps, just backwards! If a key has one flat, it is the first one in the list. If a key has two flats, these are the first two on the list, and so on.

So, a key that has four flats would have:

B♭ E♭ A♭ D♭

This key signature is A♭ major.

Hang on Barry! I read that the key of four flats was F minor.

Yes, Trudi, we are both correct. They are called relatives.

Relative major and minor

There are 13 different key signatures all together. Some have no sharps or flats; others have one to six sharps or flats. However, there are actually more keys than that because for each note you can have a major or a minor key. Each major key signature has the same number of sharps and flats as a minor key signature. They are known as the relative major and minor, like cousins!

Think back to the C major scale, which had no sharps or flats. Then we discovered the minor scale of A. That also had no sharps or flats, so C major and A minor are **relative major and minor**.

Harmony

Music would be very boring if it was all just one note at a time. The best music has lots of notes sounding at once, which gives the music different **colours** and moods. When there are several notes happening at once, we call this **harmony**. Harmonies add depth to a melody.

Using the scale of C major, we can take the first note, the third note and the fifth note to make a group of three notes. These notes are C, E and G, and playing them together makes a **chord**:

C D **E** F **G** A B C

They look like this on our music:

Notice how they stack together on top of each other, like a packet of bagels! This type of chord - one that uses notes 1, 3 and 5 - is called a **triad**, simply because it is made up of three notes. We can make a triad on any note, just by counting up to find notes 3 and 5.

> Remember these triad chords. We will be trying to play some of these on the piano later.
>
> We will also be learning about chords on the guitar!

Think back to the scales and key signatures we learnt about in the previous section. If we want to make a triad on D, we need the D major scale, which includes an F♯ on note 3, so the triad would have to be on a D, F♯ and A like this:

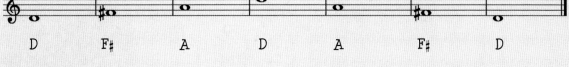

D   F#   A   D   A   F#   D

We can also try building chords on the minor scales. Let's go back to the key of D minor.

Remember that D minor has one flat in it: B♭. Notes 1, 3 and 5 are D, F and A.

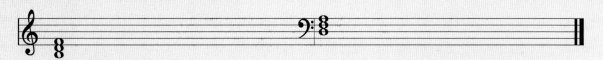

Because there is no sharp on the F, it alters the mood of the chord and like the scale makes it sound minor. So if a chord is built on the minor version of a scale, we make a **minor chord**. If we use the notes of the major scale, we have a **major chord**. Notice that the first and fifth note of a triad never change; it is the third note (the middle note) that determines the type of triad.

There are many other different types of chords, as we can add notes, such as a note 7 as well, or take notes away. Or we can add flats and sharps to the notes of chords to make many thousands of possible combinations. Chords are often played by the left hand on the piano or keyboard, or on the guitar, or by lots of instruments playing **held notes** at the same time, to accompany the tunes.

Rhythms

Oh, I love pie; my favourite is apple! What's your favourite?

So far, all the music notes we've seen have been round blobs like this:

But in fact there are many more types of note, to show sounds of different lengths. We need these to make rhythms. Music would be very boring if we couldn't make rhythms. The blob notes we have seen are worth four beats and are called **semibreves (whole notes)**. Let's imagine the semibreve is a pie – it looks a bit like one!

We can cut it into four slices, each worth a beat. These are the **crotchets (quarter notes).** They have a filled-in blob and a stick that goes up or down, called a **stem**.

We also have two-beat notes called **minims (half notes)**, which are worth half a pie, or two slices.

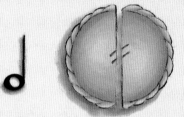

Then we have **quavers (eighth notes)**, which are worth half a beat or half a slice. These notes are fast! They hang out in pairs, which are held together with a **beam**. Sometimes we see quavers on their own, in which case they have a blob and stem and a little flicked-up **tail**.

Notes that are even faster still are **semiquavers (sixteenth notes)**, which are hard to play without practising slowly first. They are worth a quarter of a slice of pie (no one wants that slice!). Notice that they look just like quavers (eighth notes), but have a double beam.

To help us count notes and make sure they are in time, we can say certain words. For minims (half notes), we can say 'fly'. Be careful to stretch out the 'y' to make two full beats.

fly   fly

For crotchets (quarter notes), we can say 'ant'.

ant   ant   ant   ant

For quavers (eighth notes), we can say 'spider'. This word has two syllables, so say 'spi' and then 'der' for each little blob.

spi-der   spi-der   spi-der   spi-der

And for semiquavers (sixteenth notes), we can say 'caterpillar' as it has four syllables.

cat-er-pil-lar   cat-er-pil-lar   cat-er-pil-lar   cat-er-pil-lar

We can then mix these up to help us work out how any rhythm goes.

ant   spi-der   ant   spi-der   ant   ant   flyyyy!

Try tapping out that rhythm. Say the words too, and then try it without words.

Can you think of your own words using syllables for the different rhythms?

Dotted rhythms

Sometimes in music, rhythms aren't even. We may need to make a note longer and can use **dotted rhythms** to show this. If we add a dot after a note, it makes it longer than the original but shorter than the next note up. A dotted note looks like this:

Hang on! We have notes for a quarter, a half, one, two and four beats – but what about the other numbers? Is there a three-beat note?

The dot adds on half as much time again to the note. This sounds complicated, but it is quite easy when you know how to do it. We will start with a minim (half note).

We know that a minim is worth two beats. We add a dot, which is the same as half a minim (half note). The dot is worth one beat.

Two beats from the minim plus one beat from the dot makes three beats. So a **dotted minim (dotted half note)** is worth three beats.

$$\text{♩} \div 2 = \text{♪} \qquad \text{♩} + \text{♪} = 3$$

We can do the same with a crotchet (quarter note). We halve it to find the value of the dot. So, one beat divided by two is half a beat. One beat plus a half a beat is one and a half beats, so that's how much a **dotted crotchet (dotted quarter note)** is worth.

$$\text{♩} \div 2 = \text{♪} \; \tfrac{1}{2} \qquad \text{♩} + \text{♪} = 1\tfrac{1}{2} \qquad \text{♩.} = 1\tfrac{1}{2}$$

Remember our semibreve (whole note) pies? A dotted crotchet is like a slice and a half of a pie, and a dotted minim is like three-quarters of a whole pie.

Finally, let's look at a **dotted quaver (dotted eighth note)**. Remember that a quaver is worth half a beat, so the dot is worth a quarter of a beat. A half plus a quarter is three-quarters, the value of the dotted quaver.

Dotted rhythms are often paired up with a single short note to round up the number of beats.

So if you have one and a half beats from a dotted crotchet, is it often paired with a single quaver to make a full number of beats?

Exactly! And a dotted quaver (a three-quarter beat) pairs with a semiquaver (a quarter beat) to make a whole beat. They are joined together with a beam to show they are now a whole beat, like this:

A good way of counting dotted rhythms is to say the words 'long' and 'short' for the dotted rhythm:

1   a 2   a

looooooong   short

Thanks, Trudi. I will try that.

Can you work out the sums below, where we have replaced numbers with music notes?

Here's a tip to help you. Write the numbers of beats under the note first, then try the sum.

① ♩ + ♩ = ?

② ♩ + ♩ + ♩ = ?

③ ♩ + ♩ = ?

④ o − ♩ = ?

⑤ o ÷ 4 = ?

⑥ ♩ + ♩ = ?

⑦ ♩ + ♫ + ♩ = ?

⑧ o + ♩ = ?

⑨ o − ♩ = ?

⑩ ♩ ÷ 2 = ?

⑪ ♫ + ♩ = ?

⑫ ♫ + o + ♩ = ?

⑬ o − ♪ = ?

⑭ ♩ × ♩ = ?

Time and bars

Do you remember that we talked about bars when we were looking at the stave? They are the signposts that tell us where we are in the music. They are set out at regular intervals, so we can see where the strong beats in the music fall. We mark each bar with a **bar line**, like this:

Most music has four beats in a bar. We describe this as **common time** and we put a bar line after every four beats. Common time is also called **4/4 time**. This is a **time signature** and sets the feel of the beats for the whole piece. Every time signature has two numbers. The top number tells us how many beats or counts there are in each bar and the bottom number tells us what type of beats they are, such as minims (half notes) or crotchets (quarter notes).

So in 4/4 time we have bars worth four crotchets (quarter notes). To fill each bar we need a semibreve (whole note) or a pie! We can then divide the bar (or cut the pie) however we like to make up a rhythm.

There are many more time signatures. Some common ones are 3/4 time, which is the same as 4/4 time but with three beats in a bar. It has a more dance-like feel, and is the time signature used for waltzes.

Another time signature is 6/8 time, which is different because instead of counting in crotchet (quarter note) beats, we count in quaver (eighth note) beats. Therefore there are six quaver (eighth note) beats in a bar. This time signature skips along and is used a lot in folk music, which we will learn more about in Chapter 4.

Add the bar lines

Count how long each note is, then add the bar line after the correct number of beats for the time signature.

Notice how much easier it is to follow the music with the bar lines than without!

Tempo

Have you ever had your pulse taken? You can feel your blood rushing around your body, keeping a steady beat. Music has a pulse too: the beats we count when we clap out rhythms. The pulse of music can be fast, just like our heartbeat after we have been running, or slow, like our heartbeat when we are lying down. The difference in speed is what we call **tempo**.

What sort of tempo would suit a funeral march? What about a dance track?

If our metronome mark is crotchet = 60 bpm, how many seconds long is each crotchet? What about crotchet = 120 bpm?

Did you know?

We can measure tempo in beats per minute (bpm). So at the beginning of the music it is useful to have a symbol to tell us how many of a particular type of note there are in a minute.

If you see 'M.M.' written on the music, before the number of beats per minute, it means 'Maelzel's Metronome'. Johann Nepomuk Maelzel was a German man who invented the first **metronome** machine 200 years ago. Metronomes click quickly or slowly to count beats for you. They are very useful for practising music, as you can get the rhythms perfectly in time. (There are free apps for this too, so why not download one?)

The elements of music

The **elements of music** are all the main features that make up a piece of music. So far we have looked at:

𝄞 **Pitch** How high or low the music is, where the notes sit on the stave, and which clef we use.

𝄞 **Melody** The way we stick different notes or pitches together to make tunes.

𝄞 **Rhythm** The number of beats in a bar and the length each note is, in order to make interesting patterns.

𝄞 **Harmony** and **tonality** The chords in a piece and whether it is based on a major scale or a minor scale or neither.

𝄞 **Tempo** How fast or slow the music is.

Getting the right notes in the right places to form a piece of music seems like the most important thing, doesn't it? But without some other elements, music could get very boring and would all end up sounding the same.

A good way to stop music sounding boring is by using **dynamics**. This just means making the music loud or quiet, and it can change throughout the piece to highlight certain melodies, to build tension and drama, or to make us jump!

Did you know?

An Austrian composer called Joseph Haydn wrote a famous symphony (see Chapter 4) called the *Surprise Symphony*. He wrote it whilst he was visiting London in 1791 and the orchestras and audiences there loved it.

In one movement (part) of the music, the tune started quietly and simply. Then, suddenly, out of nowhere there was one really loud note from the whole orchestra, and it made the audience jump out of their seats! Then it carried on quietly as though nothing had happened. The musicians in the orchestra laughed as they saw the audience's faces.

Haydn was famous for writing these little jokes into his music. Many composers continue to do this to this day!

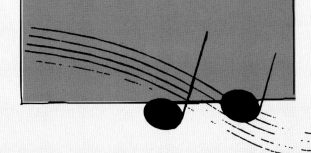

Dynamics: loud and quiet

Earlier, we learnt that Italian words are used to describe music. The Italian words for the different dynamics are below. In written music, there often isn't room to write the whole word so just the main letters are used to show the **performer** how loud to play in that place:

- **Pianissimo** Very quiet *(pp)*
- **Piano** Quiet *(p)*
- **Mezzo piano** Fairly quiet *(mp)*
- **Mezzo forte** Fairly loud *(mf)*
- **Forte** Strong and loud *(f)*
- **Fortissimo** Very loud *(ff)*

These instructions are all great if, like Haydn's 'Surprise', it is important to change the volume suddenly. That happens a lot in music, but we can also slowly increase or decrease the volume too. We call this **crescendo** *(cres.* or *cresc.)* - gradually getting louder, or **diminuendo** *(dim.)* - gradually getting quieter.

These are long words so we can also use symbols to show the volume changes. The symbols are like V-shapes lying on their sides and mean 'more than' and 'less than'. Think of a crocodile's mouth. Where it is fully open, the sound is loudest and where his jaw is, the sound is quietest. In the left-hand picture, the sound is going from quiet to loud. In the right-hand picture, the sound is going from loud to quiet.

LOUD!

quiet   crescendo   diminuendo   quiet

<   >

Pink elephants

This is a great game for practising dynamics. All you need is a friend! One friend is enough, but you could use several standing in a circle. Take it in turns to be the leader.

The leader stands in the middle of the circle (or in front, if there are just two or three of you). Everyone else starts chanting: 'Pink elephants, pink elephants!' Now the leader decides on the dynamics for the chant, making a signal to tell everyone what to do.

If the leader crouches down, it means pianissimo (very quiet), so everyone has to whisper the chant. If she touches her knees, it means mezzo piano (fairly quiet), so everyone chants in their normal speaking voice. If she taps her shoulders, it means mezzo forte (fairly loud) and everyone has to chant the words quite loudly – imagine you're outside or calling someone across the room. If she puts her hands in the air, it means forte (loud), so everyone has to shout. If she jumps up and down, it means fortissimo (very loud), so everyone can raise the roof!

If you have instruments, play with these. The rhythm is:

pink   el - e - phants

Structure

The **structure** of a piece of music, just like the structure of a house, is what holds it together and gives it an outline. Different types of music have different structure patterns, like different buildings have different structures.

For example, a pop song often uses a verse-chorus structure something like this:

Introduction - Verse - Chorus - Verse - Chorus - Bridge - Chorus - Verse - End

The **introduction** sets the mood and style of the song. The **verse** introduces the song's themes. The **chorus** is the catchy tune with the main message of the song. The chorus doesn't change; the verses are similar to each other but usually have different words. The **bridge** is a bit of different music, still in the same style, to break up the repetitiveness of the chorus. Often, it makes a feature of an instrument, such as the guitar, and gives the singer a break.

A piece of music for an orchestra often uses a **symphony** structure. This is a large piece of music made up of four **movements**. These are mini pieces that are different in mood, but in the same style as all the others. Together they make up one big piece of music. There are gaps between movements, where the musicians turn over their music or pick up different instruments as necessary, but usually people wait until the end of the whole piece to applaud. There is a traditional structure for movements, shown above,right although there are many variations:

First movement Fast in tempo and introduces all the main themes and **home key** of the symphony.

Second movement Slow and often sad in mood.

Third movement Often a dance style, with skipping rhythms or musical jokes.

Fourth movement The finale, which revisits the main tunes. It is often fast and happy in mood.

There are many sub-structures too, to help the composer fit tunes into each movement, although these have changed through time as fashions have changed. We will learn more about this in Chapter 4.

Why don't you listen to a pop song and an orchestral symphony and see if you can spot the different sections of the structure?

Binary and ternary structures

Some of the best musical structures are really simple, such as **binary** and **ternary forms**. 'Binary' means 'two parts', so it is just two different tunes in one piece. First we hear one tune, which we can call part A. When that tune is finished, we hear another tune, which is different but in the same style, which we call part B. It is a piece of two halves:

A-B

Sometimes, both parts are repeated to make the music a bit longer:

AA-BB

'Ternary' means 'three parts'. There are two tunes again, parts A and B, just like before. For the third part, tune A comes back and often it is changed a little bit, just to make it more interesting. We would write it like this:

A-B-A2

Texture

Another element of music is **texture**. Normally, we use this word to describe the feel and thickness of materials. It has a similar meaning in music: texture is all about the layers in the music.

For example a **solo**, where one musician plays or sings one line of music on her own, is a very thin texture, like a single slice of bread.

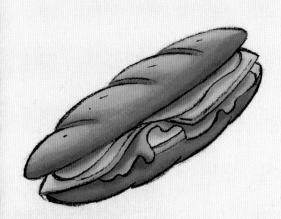

If we put some butter on the bread, it would be like adding a layer to the music. This could be a **duet**, where two musicians play together. Just like butter goes with bread, the two musicians sound different but go together and complement each other.

The more different lines of music that are added, the thicker and more complicated the music gets, like adding cheese and ham to the buttered bread to make a sandwich. Everyone has different parts to play, which weave in and out of each other and complement each other. Cheese and ham are very different foods, but they taste good together!

Sometimes in large groups of musicians, such as an orchestra or band, all the musicians play the same tune. We call this playing in **unison**. The music sounds thicker than a solo, but there's still only one line of music happening. So in our sandwich, we have no butter or cheese or ham, but we have lots and lots of bread!

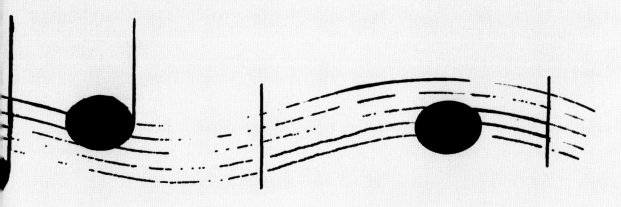

Writing music

When composers write music, they come up with little ideas - maybe a melody or rhythm or the style of a piece - and then think how best to write them down using the elements.

Musicians would call their first composed piece of music Opus 1! How many more compositions can you come up with?

Composer lab

Writing your own piece of music is like being a scientist and mixing chemicals and processes to make a new product. We have to think about all the basic materials we are going to use, imagine what the final product will look like, and then mix the materials together carefully to make the product.

You will need:

• Musical instruments, or voices, or a computer with GarageBand or other music program on

• Something to record yourself with

• A big piece of paper and some coloured pens

• Lots of friends to help you

Start by writing down all the musical elements on the paper. Then work out how you want the song to be for each element. For example, do you want the tempo to be fast or slow or something in-between? Are you going to use a song structure or an A-B-type structure? Do you want to use high notes and sounds or low notes and sounds? Do you want it to be loud or quiet?

Now all you need to do is come up with a fantastic tune! This is where you work out the melody and rhythm. Try out different notes on the instruments or using the computer (remember the things you learned earlier) and find notes that sound good together. Then repeat it over and over to use as the main tune or chorus, depending on which structure you've chosen.

Practise the piece, then record it and play it back to listen to it. Congratulations! You've written your first piece of music.

Timbre

The last element we need to think about is **timbre**. Timbre is the tone or sound quality of an instrument. For example, a violin doesn't sound the same as a trumpet. They could be playing the same tune, but you would hear the difference. If a man sang a song and a woman sang a song, their voices would sound different. Different people like different timbres and people often choose to play an instrument or listen to a type of music that uses particular instruments because of how they sound.

Time to learn about all the different instruments, I think.

Yes, Barry. I wonder which one will be my favourite.

I like the double bass or the bass guitar as they share my name!

Great! I want to learn about the flute. That's a high instrument, isn't it? Let's find out!

2
MUSICAL INSTRUMENTS

Instruments are grouped into families based on their features. The most important features are how an instrument produces sound and the materials it is made of. You can often guess which instruments belong together, as they sound similar. Just like real families, they often look alike too, and have similar shapes.

Woodwind

Our first family is the woodwind family. As you can guess from the name, they are traditionally made of wood, but there are some exceptions, as we will see later on. However, all of the woodwind instruments have one thing in common - you use air from your lungs to blow into them through your lips, and a sound is made! You then use your fingers to press down keys and cover holes to make the notes.

To learn how to play the recorder and for some tunes to try, turn to page 96

Recorder

The recorder is one of the oldest musical instruments. It is made out of wood (though some, like the ones you may have in your school, are made out of plastic). You simply blow into the top end to make a sound. However, if you don't blow carefully, it will squeak and make a horrid noise.

If it is played properly, the recorder can sound beautiful. Recorder-like instruments are found all over the world, so it is very popular. It sounds 'woody' and very natural, and is easy to listen to.

The recorder was considered a very important instrument in medieval times and was played for most major events, such as weddings, funerals, feasts and parties, and worship. It became slightly less popular as other instruments, such as the flute and oboe, were invented. However, in the early twentieth century, musicians decided to try and discover more old pieces of music and play them as they would have been played hundreds of years before. This led to more people deciding to play the recorder. Also, composers began to write solos for the recorder in more modern styles, to see how much the recorder could do.

You may be used to seeing just one size of recorder, but there are many! The ones most people play are the descant (like the ones in school), or the treble, which is a bit bigger. Other recorders are the tiny sopranino, which is only about 24 cm (9½ in) long, to the contrabass, which is over 1 m (39 in) tall - imagine that!

Flute

The flute started out as a wooden instrument. It was very similar to the recorder. You hold it sideways, rather than down like a recorder. Over the years, people decided to make metal flutes, which sounded louder. Instead of blowing straight down into the flute, you purse your lips and blow over the hole. It's just like blowing over an empty bottle – can you do that?

Unlike a recorder, which just has holes, a flute has **keys**. You press the keys down with your fingers, which makes **pads** cover the holes. There are many more keys than we have fingers! Flute players keep their fingers over certain keys. You start with your left hand at the top, just like the recorder, but instead of putting your first finger on the first hole, you skip the first little key entirely. Look at the diagram on the next page: the pink spots are where the fingers of your left hand go (as well as your thumb on the back) and the yellow spots are where the fingers of your right hand go.

Bottle-flutes

You will need:
- Clean plastic bottles, different sizes
- Water
- Food colourings
- A pen that will write on plastic
- An adult to help you

You can practise making 'flute lips' by blowing over bottle tops. This is fun, but it is even more fun to make different notes and sounds. Start by experimenting with the different-sized bottles. The bigger ones make a lower sound than the smaller ones. Now fill the bottles with water to make the space in them smaller and the note higher. Try this with one bottle first, by filling it up and blowing over the rim, then gradually tip water out so it contains less. Once you've found a note you like, make another bottle, with a different note. Put a drop of different food dye in each so you can tell them apart. Can you make up a piece of music on your new bottle-flutes?

If you're really clever, you could try and make a scale. Get an adult to help you make exact pitch notes by using a **tuner**, a machine that measures pitch.

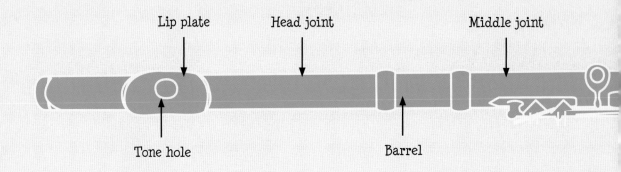

Lip plate   Head joint   Middle joint

Tone hole   Barrel

I can see that there are four keys for the right hand to play.

Some notes on the flute use the extra little keys at the bottom and sticking out the side, Barry, but nearly every note on the flute uses the bottom key in the right hand.

So we hold down our little finger for nearly every note? We don't do that with a recorder!

That's right, Barry. But remember, the flute has lots of keys, rather than just holes.

Did you know?

The oldest instruments were made from hollowed-out bones with holes punched through them. They were an early type of flutes or recorder. Some of the earliest were made from mammoths' bones, and some have been found that are over 42,000 years old!

Foot joint

You can get different types of flute, such as the alto or bass flute. These are bigger than a regular flute, but are quite rare. However, lots and lots of flute players will also have a **piccolo**. A piccolo is a baby flute that is half the size of a normal flute and sounds one octave higher, so it is very squeaky and needs a good player to make it sound pretty. It is the highest-sounding musical instrument there is, so there is normally only one in an orchestra or band. It can easily be heard floating above everyone else!

Clarinet

The clarinet is basically a long wooden tube with holes in it, like a recorder, but it has an extra part at the top where you blow into it to produce the sound. We call this bit the **mouthpiece**. The mouthpiece includes a **reed**, which is strapped to it with a **ligature**. A reed is a flat bit of wood, which has been cut and scraped to size. When we blow over it, it vibrates to make a sound. Reeds come in different sizes to fit different types of woodwind instrument, and in different strengths depending on how good the player is and what sort of sound he wants to make.

To protect the reed from the clarinet player's teeth, the musician (called a **clarinettist**) rolls his bottom lip in and over his teeth and bites down on the top of the plastic mouthpiece with his top teeth.

Clarinet thumb

Wash your hands, because you are going to put your fingers in your mouth!

To practise how to play a clarinet, you need to make sure it goes into your mouth properly.

Make a thumbs-up sign with your thumb. Turn your thumb so the nail is against your bottom lip. Roll your thumb back so the tip is in your mouth. Now bite down on the fleshy pad of your thumb tip with your two front teeth. If you bite so hard that you hurt your thumb, that's too much pressure to play. The grip should be firm, but not tight.

That's it! You're ready to play the clarinet.

Clarinets are made out of African hardwood, though clarinets for beginners are often made out of plastic, as this is much cheaper. Both types have a distinctive 'woody' sound, which can be very low and earthy (in what we call the **chalumeau register**) or high and piercing.

A clarinet also has keys on it, which are usually made out of silver metal. The keys don't cover the main finger holes, but form a circle around them. There are lots of extra keys down the sides of the clarinet, which are played with the sides of your fingers. It looks complicated, but clarinettists get used to where their fingers are meant to go to play each note.

All these keys give the clarinet one of the biggest ranges (the gap between the lowest and highest note) of all the woodwind instruments. The player also has to anticipate how to blow the note, so he has to blow properly and with his lips tightened just right, otherwise it will squeak. For example, the clarinettist has to blow a bit differently depending on whether it is a low note or a high note.

The clarinet is a **transposing instrument**. That means that when you press your fingers down to make a C note, it doesn't sound like a C on the piano, or on a tuner. So the music for a clarinettist needs to have a different key signature to that of the other instruments, to make the notes match up. Most clarinets are in the key of B♭, which means that when you press your fingers down to make a C, it sounds like a B♭ on the piano. Some people also have clarinets in A, and when you press the same fingers down to play a C, it sounds even lower.

Mini clarinets sound even higher and can be very piercing and squeaky in their sound. These clarinets are in E♭. Bass clarinets are in B♭ but are twice as big as a regular clarinet. These make a very low and breathy sound.

A bass clarinet player reads music off the treble clef. This is because the **fingerings** for the notes are exactly the same as for a regular clarinet; it's just the way it sounds that is different. This system means it is easy for a clarinettist to change between different types of clarinet. Someone who started learning on a normal B♭ clarinet would therefore be able to play all the different types of clarinets. We call these instruments **subsidiary instruments**.

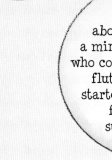

I didn't know there was a bass clarinet! Does that mean you read bass clef music?

Do you remember learning about the piccolo, which is a mini flute? Because a person who could play piccolo could play flute as well, and probably started out by learning on the flute, that makes it a subsidiary instrument too!

Grass reeds

You will need:
- Some freshly cut long grass
- Scissors
- An adult to help you

WARNING! Please make sure all grass is thoroughly washed before putting it near your mouth!

Take a thick blade of grass and cut the ends off squarely to make a rectangle. Place the grass between the knuckles of both

your thumbs, keeping it straight. Squeeze the top of your thumbs together to trap it. This should leave a little gap with the grass suspended in the middle of it.

Now put your lips to the hole between your thumbs and blow through it. It should make a squeaky, buzzy noise! This is exactly how reeds work on clarinets, oboes, bassoons and saxophones, which we will be looking at soon.

Oboe

The oboe looks a lot like the clarinet and sometimes people get them confused, because they are both in black wood with lots of silver keys. Oboes for beginners are plastic, and advanced and professional players use ones made of African hardwood. The oboe uses reeds too, but instead of sticking them on a mouthpiece, two reeds are tied together and are placed directly between the player's lips. This is called a double reed and like the clarinet, the oboe player (called an oboist) rolls her lips over her teeth to avoid biting the reed, but she has to do this with both lips!

The oboe is used to 'tune up' an orchestra or band. This is because it has a very clear and piercing tone, which most of the musicians will be able to hear easily. Also, the oboe normally sits right in the middle of the orchestra or wind band (see Chapter 3). The oboe (like the flute and recorder) is in C (**concert pitch**), unlike the clarinet. However, the note most people use to tune their instruments is an A.

Did you know?

There is a piece of music written by the famous film music composer Ennio Morricone called 'Gabriel's Oboe' from a 1986 film called *The Mission*. It is a really famous tune and people love it so much that it has been recorded by nearly every instrument, and set to words for singers. It even won an Academy Award and Golden Globe for the Best Original Score in the big film prize ceremonies.

Cor anglais

There is also a big, oboe-like instrument people called a *cor anglais*, which literally means 'English horn'. But it isn't a horn at all and was first used in Central Europe, so it isn't English either! It is used a lot for solos as it has a very distinctive sound. A famous example is the second movement of Czechoslovakian composer Dvorak's Symphony No. 9 'The New World'.

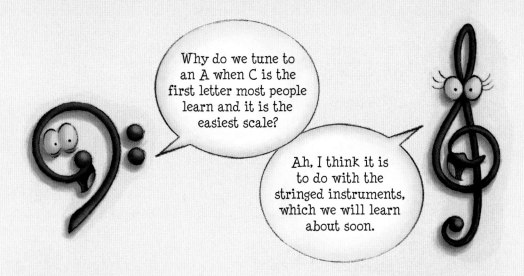

Why do we tune to an A when C is the first letter most people learn and it is the easiest scale?

Ah, I think it is to do with the stringed instruments, which we will learn about soon.

Bassoon

The bassoon is a double-reed instrument, like the oboe, but it is much bigger. It is usually made with maple wood, which is stained to give a range of colours from yellow-brown to red and dark brown. The instrument is like a big, long stick that the player (called a bassoonist) either has to prop up on a stick called a **spike** or hang from a strap around his neck or shoulders. Then he holds the bassoon diagonally across his body and blows in the mouthpiece, which sticks out on a long metal pipe called a **crook**. The bassoon looks rather like a giant praying mantis! Like all the woodwind instruments, you place your left hand at the top.

The bassoon is the biggest and lowest sounding of the woodwind family and has a rather solemn sound. There is even a giant bassoon called a **contrabassoon**, which sounds one octave lower! Because the bassoon is so big and a little more complicated than the other wind instruments, people usually start on another reed instrument such as the saxophone, clarinet or oboe, before moving to bassoon when they are a bit older and bigger.

When playing the bassoon, the double reed is placed between rolled-up lips, which must not flop about. To do this, you form your lips into an O-shape, and then roll them inwards. But then to get a big sound and control the air, you need to relax your jaw and sigh down into a yawn, without moving your lips. It is hard to get your muscles all working in the right way to make the sound, but bassoonists get used to this. Practising the instrument and doing exercises away from the instrument makes your lip muscles very strong and then they can always form the right shape. The shape you hold your lips in to play certain wind or brass instruments is called your **embouchure**.

The bassoon is the only wind instrument to play in the bass clef, so it's my favourite already!

If you think about it, our lips form thousands of different shapes every day to make words when we speak.

Yes, Trudi, and we don't find that hard. We don't even think about it! Because we have been using our lips to talk since we were babies, it has become a habit.

So, if we practise getting the right embouchure for our instrument, and practise a lot, our lips will move by habit, and it won't be hard work.

Exactly, Trudi!

Saxophone

The saxophone is the youngest woodwind instrument. It was invented in 1840 to fill the gap between the quieter woodwind instruments and the clumsier brass families. People sometimes get confused about which family the saxophone is in, because it's made out of shiny metal, like all brass instruments. But it uses a mouthpiece and a reed, like a clarinet, to make a sound. The way a sound is made is more important in deciding on the family that an instrument belongs to than the material it is made of (remember most flutes are metal nowadays).

Saxophones have a powerful sound that is used a lot in jazz music, though you can also find saxophones in military music and sometimes in the orchestra, too. They are really popular and fun to play. You press down keys to make the notes, just like on the flute. A lot of people who play saxophone also play a woodwind instrument - usually the flute (because the fingers match) or clarinet (because the mouthpieces match).

Sax spotting

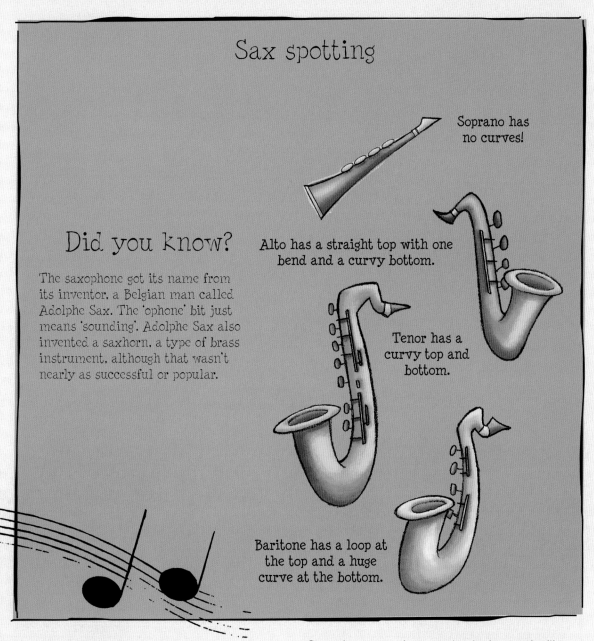

Soprano has no curves!

Alto has a straight top with one bend and a curvy bottom.

Tenor has a curvy top and bottom.

Baritone has a loop at the top and a huge curve at the bottom.

Did you know?

The saxophone got its name from its inventor, a Belgian man called Adolphe Sax. The 'ophone' bit just means 'sounding'. Adolphe Sax also invented a saxhorn, a type of brass instrument, although that wasn't nearly as successful or popular.

The saxophone comes in many different sizes, so some can play really high notes and some can play really low notes. The most common type is the alto saxophone, whose sound is in the middle. Higher ones are called soprano and sopranino, and lower ones are called tenor and baritone. There are even saxophone 'choirs' in which all the saxophones play at once in beautiful harmonies!

Saxophones are transposing instruments, like the clarinet. They follow the same pattern of keys, with some saxophones in B♭ (soprano and tenor) and some in E♭ (sopranino, alto and baritone). This means a saxophone player only has to learn one set of fingerings for all the notes. Once you can play one saxophone, you can play all of them. However, it takes a lot of practice to get your lips and the way you blow right on the different sizes of mouthpiece, in order to make a good sound.

Brass

All brass instruments get their name from the fact that they were once all made of... brass! Brass is a type of metal, although today lots of different types of metal are used to make the instruments. Members of the brass family of instruments are all very similar in the way the player makes the sound. They have a little metal cup that goes into the top of the instrument, called a mouthpiece, which you blow into. You put your lips against the mouthpiece and make them vibrate. You do this by blowing a raspberry, but in a controlled way.

As the sound vibrates through the metal tube, it becomes louder. The way we purse our lips to blow the controlled raspberry is called an embouchure, as for a wind instrument. The same basic embouchure is needed for all brass instruments, but is a different size depending on how big the instrument is.

Buzzy faces

Challenge! Can you buzz the national anthem just on your lips? This is hard, but give it a try.

You will need:
* A clean straw
* A mirror
* A strong cardboard or plastic tube

Before you start, please make sure the tube is clean, as you are going to put your face on it.

Place the straw between your lips and suck on it as if you were drinking. Now turn the sucking action around and blow instead. However, you must only let air escape through the straw. Open your mouth to breathe as needed, and then carry on blowing down the straw. Look at the shape your lips are making in the mirror. Notice how the muscles at the corners of your mouth are pursed together and there are lines around your mouth. This is good!

We are going to use these muscles to make the buzzing sound.

If you're not sure how to buzz, practise blowing raspberries with your lips first. The louder and wetter the better! Now purse your lips to control the buzz into a point at the centre of your lips. To do this, keep blowing but pull the straw out of your mouth. Turn the blow into a buzz. Practise this a few times. You should sound like a loud, buzzing fly.

Now try placing this buzz against the tube. Notice how the sound suddenly gets fuller and louder as you buzz. This is how brass instruments work!

Experiment with squeezing and relaxing your lip muscles to make different notes. Can you make a high-, middle- and low-sounding buzz? Can you buzz the tune of the national anthem?

Brass players change notes by moving their lips into different positions, from very tight to very relaxed. The more that the muscles of the face are squeezed together, the higher the note will be. Watch out, though, because it is the pressure between the lips themselves and not between the lips and the mouthpiece that is important. If you press the hard metal mouthpiece on to your lips too hard, the noise will stop. It will also hurt.

Trumpet

The trumpet is the most famous and most versatile of the brass family of instruments. It is found in almost every type of music, including jazz, Latin, pop and military music, as well as being a very important member of the orchestra. Trumpets are loud and have a bright sound. Depending on the instrument and player, they can sound really mellow and sultry, like in a jazz ballad; funky and upbeat, like in a dance track; angry and driving, like in a big orchestral symphony; or really haunting, like in a military fanfare. There is nothing you cannot do with a trumpet!

The trumpet is a transposing instrument and there are lots of different kinds. They include the piccolo trumpet, which is tiny and plays very high notes. The most common kind is the trumpet in B♭, but there is also a trumpet in E♭ (which is smaller and higher), D, C, F and A. Giant trumpets, which sound really low, are called bass trumpets. These are normally played by trombonists or euphonium players (we will look at these instruments soon). This is because they are so big that they have a big mouthpiece, which is close to a trombone mouthpiece in size, and therefore needs a player with a big embouchure.

There are subsidiary instruments for the trumpet, too. These are very similar to the trumpet, with the same keys and notes, but are slightly different shapes. They are the **cornet** and the **flugelhorn**.

trumpet

cornet and flugelhorn

These instruments look different from the side but the shape of the tube is a bit different to that of the trumpet, too. If we unravelled a trumpet, it would be one long, straight tube in a cone shape, until the end, where it flares out. An unravelled cornet or flugelhorn would be a very long cone, which gets bigger very gradually.

This shape makes the sound more mellow and 'fluffy'. The cornet is used in military pieces and brass band music to play the melodies and blend with the other brass instruments, whilst the flugelhorn is often used for beautiful ballads in jazz and brass band music.

A long time ago, the trumpet didn't have the three buttons, known as valves, that we are used to today. It was just a long tube looped together, with a mouthpiece in the small end. But the player could still play certain notes of a scale by changing the pressure of his lips. The main ones were 1, 3 and 5. This formed the basis of fanfares, which we can still hear played by soldiers today. You can play these fanfares on a modern trumpet, too, without pressing any valves.

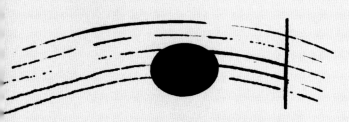

How come the trumpet only has three valves? Flutes and clarinets have lots of keys.

All brass instruments only have three or four valves, Trudi. The player can change her lips to play all the notes, so each finger combination can play many different notes.

French horn

The French horn is the only brass instrument you stick your hand in the end of! This gives it a unique sound that is different to other brass instruments. This means that it blends really well with stringed and wind instruments, as well as brass, and it was the first brass instrument to be added to the orchestra because of this.

The French horn is a very old instrument. Like the trumpet, at one time it didn't have any valves, but was just one very long, curly tube. The horn player would have to carry a range of end tubes, called crooks, of different lengths. This would enable her to play pieces in any key the piece required. So if she were playing a piece in D major, she would have to find the crook that made the D sound.

Modern French horns have valves, just like the trumpet. However, they are unusual because almost everyone nowadays plays a horn with **rotary valves**, which look like this:

This is instead of **piston valves**, which are on the trumpet, cornet and flugelhorn and look like this:

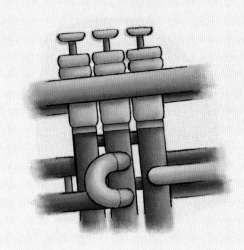

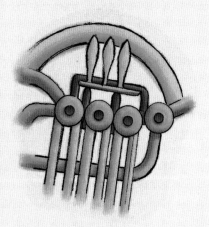

Both types of valve do the same job. Some people think that each makes a slightly different sound. In Britain and the USA, most brass players have instruments with piston valves. In mainland Europe, rotary valves are more common on tubas and trumpets as well as horns.

French horns sound really regal and important, with a clear sound that can soar above the orchestra or band. They also have a really big range, meaning they can play very low and very high - more than most brass and woodwind instruments. Most people start on a single horn, but may progress to a double horn. This is basically two horns in one. There are two different lengths of tube, one tuned to an F note and one tuned to a B♭ note. The player swaps between them by using a valve pressed by her thumb, and so can play many notes.

Tuba

The tuba is the biggest instrument in the brass family. It is made of metal, and comes in lots of different versions and keys. Most tubas have a fourth button, or valve, which is used to make certain notes more in tune and to play lower notes than the trumpet can.

Professional tuba players (called **tubists**) will have several different tubas that they will play on different occasions, depending on the music they are playing. They will follow the tradition of the **ensemble** or composer.

The tuba has a fantastic deep and booming sound and it can be played really loudly or really quietly. It does not often get the chance to play solos, because it sounds so low.

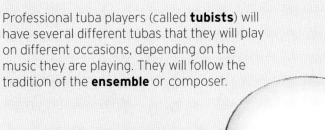

I love tubas because they're low like me!

Yes Barry, tubas definitely play in bass clef. Their notes are so low that a lot of them hang off the bottom of the bass clef!

Euphonium

The euphonium is also known as a tenor tuba and is the little brother of the tuba. It looks exactly the same but is a little bit smaller and sounds a bit higher. Euphoniums have a fourth valve and almost all of them are in B♭, like the most popular trumpet and clarinet, but sounding an octave lower.

Euphoniums are known for their beautiful deep tone and often play solos. They play in brass bands all the time and often take the lead melodies. They are also used a lot in military and wind bands, as well as in European folk music, such as in **oompah bands**. They are rarely used in orchestras but when they are, they often play stunning solo parts.

Although the euphonium sounds low, at the same pitch as a trombone (which we will look at soon), most euphonium players will read treble clef music. Euphoniums are in B♭, so they read music in the same key as a clarinet in B♭ and trumpet in B♭, but they sound exactly an octave lower. This makes the euphonium an **octave-transposing instrument**. Other examples include the bass clarinet and the double bass. We will look more at this later.

Tenor (alto) and baritone (tenor) horns

These horns are members of the tuba family, so they are basically baby tubas! They are even smaller than the euphonium and mostly have just three valves. The horns are famous for having really mellow, beautiful sounds. They are mostly used in marching and brass bands, as they blend very well with the other brass instruments. The horns are transposing instruments. The tenor (alto) horn is higher and smaller and is in E♭, whilst the bigger baritone (tenor) horn is in B♭.

Trombone

The trombone is the odd one out in the brass family, as the notes are not produced by valves. Instead a long tube, known as the **slide**, is moved in and out. The player, known as a **trombonist**, has to learn where the notes are on the slide. However, it is easier than it sounds, as there are seven basic slide '**positions**' for the different notes. The trombonist gets used to where he needs to put his arm to produce the required note.

Trombones are low, so read music off me, the bass clef.

Hello Barry, I'm Tom Tenor, remember me? A lot of music for trombone uses music written on me, the tenor clef!

This is because trombones are not as low as tubas, so a lot of their notes fall above middle C, and therefore hang off the top of you, Barry!

So using the tenor clef means there is more room for slightly higher notes that aren't high enough for the treble or alto clef. Other instruments that use me include the bassoon and the cello. These instruments are often called tenor instruments. Often, the trombone is called the tenor trombone.

Because trombones do not need valves to make all the notes, they were used for melodies and tunes long before the trumpet and the horn. However, they joined the orchestra much later. Trombones are now a very important part of the brass section in every orchestra, brass band, jazz band, wind band, military band and marching band, as well as being a big part of a lot of European folk music. They can be heard on almost every film score, and are being used more and more in pop music, too. Trombones can do almost everything!

Trombones are especially famous for their swoopy sound, where they go from high to low, or low to high by moving the slide slowly between the positions. This is called a **glissando**. Trombones can sound really jazzy, or loud and piercing, or beautiful and mellow; they are very expressive! In the past, trombones were considered to make such a holy and beautiful sound that they were only heard in sacred church music for hundreds of years.

Trombones are low instruments, sounding the same as euphoniums and just a bit higher than the tuba. However, they read music at concert pitch. This is the opposite of transposing instruments, so when a trombonist plays a C, it sounds just like the C on the piano. All instruments that don't transpose are concert pitch instruments, such as the flute, oboe, bassoon and piano (also all the stringed instruments, which we will look at in the next section).

A regular trombone is called a tenor trombone, but there are also alto and bass varieties. The alto trombone is a bit smaller and higher and may be played by a tenor trombonist as a subsidiary instrument. But the bass trombone is different instrument. It is the same pitch as the tenor trombone, but it is better at playing lower notes because it has extra length of tube in the top end and is bigger and wider. It has a deep and piercing sound and can play very loudly.

I like the bass trombone! It only uses the bass clef.

No, the tenor is definitely best!

Strings

Stringed instruments are easy to recognize, with pretty, curvy shapes, long strings, and a really wide range of beautiful sounds. Depending on how you pluck, strum or rub the strings, you can make so many different sounds. Stringed instruments have been around for a very long time and have an interesting history. They formed the very first orchestras (before woodwind, brass and percussion) and are very popular solo instruments - soloists often show off how fast and brilliantly they can play them.

The main four stringed instruments are the violin, viola, cello and double bass. These are called the orchestral strings or **bowed strings**

(we will learn more about this later). Then we have the harp, which is played in orchestras but is also used as a solo instrument a lot too. Finally, the guitar - which is a bit different to the others - is probably the most famous stringed instrument!

Stringed instruments are different to wind and brass instruments: none of them is a transposing instrument; they are all at concert pitch. All stringed instruments use **conventional tuning**. This means their notes sound exactly as the same note on a piano would, and the players read music at the pitch they sound.

Violin

The violin is the smallest of the stringed instruments. Even so, people make baby versions of violins for children, such as a three-quarter size or a half size, or even a quarter size, which is tiny, like a toy! As long as you can hold a violin up, you can play a note on it and some people start playing the violin as soon as they can walk, at about two years old! It doesn't matter how old you are, though, it's never too old to learn. The violin gets to play some of the best music ever written. When it is in an orchestra or a smaller ensemble, such as a **string quartet**, it gets most of the tunes and solos. Violins are played a lot in folk and pop music, too.

The violin is held on your left shoulder and tucked under the chin, and the bit with the strings points out and away from you. To play it, you press the strings with your left hand to form the notes, while drawing a bow (held in your right hand) across it at different angles to make the sound.

It has four strings, which are ever so slightly different in thickness. The thickest string should be on the left side as you hold the violin up, and the strings get thinner to the right. The strings are slightly curved over the black strip (**fingerboard** - look at the diagram on page 63). This is so you can play just one or two strings at a time to make a tune. (This is different to a guitar, which has flat strings, so they can all be played at once to make chords.) The strings have different pitches to make the following notes:

G D A E

You can remember this by making up a rhyme, like the one we used for the notes on the stave.

Try:

Green **D**ragons **A**re **E**normous

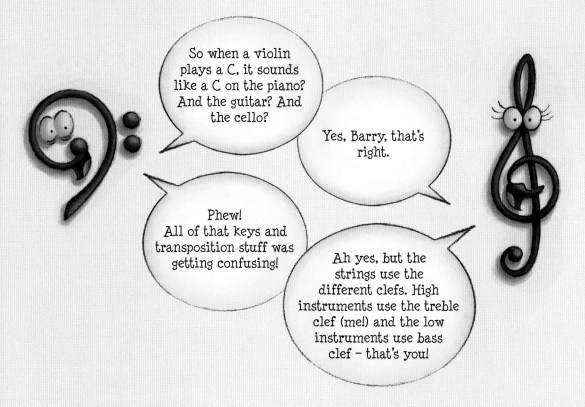

So when a violin plays a C, it sounds like a C on the piano? And the guitar? And the cello?

Yes, Barry, that's right.

Phew! All of that keys and transposition stuff was getting confusing!

Ah yes, but the strings use the different clefs. High instruments use the treble clef (me!) and the low instruments use bass clef – that's you!

Air violin

I'm sure you've heard of air guitar – now you can try air violin! It is a really fun way of dancing round the house and joining in with your favourite instrumental music. You could even invite some friends and make an air orchestra!

Start by standing up tall with your feet together, like a soldier. Then bend your feet outwards, like a penguin. Take a step forward with your left foot, and bring your left arm up, with the palm of your hand facing upwards. Make sure your elbow is bent and your wrist is all relaxed and floppy. Bring the top of your right wrist up near your nose, then throw your arm away again. Repeat: in and out again and again... you're playing air violin now!

Now that you look like a violin player, add a backing track. Some great violin pieces to jam along to are:

Eine Kleine Nachtmusik, Allegro by Wolfgang Amadeus Mozart

The Four Seasons by Antonio Vivaldi

Palladio by Karl Jenkins

Libertango by Astor Piazzolla

Look them up on YouTube or Spotify and get moving!

Can you think up your own rhyme to remember the letters of the strings?

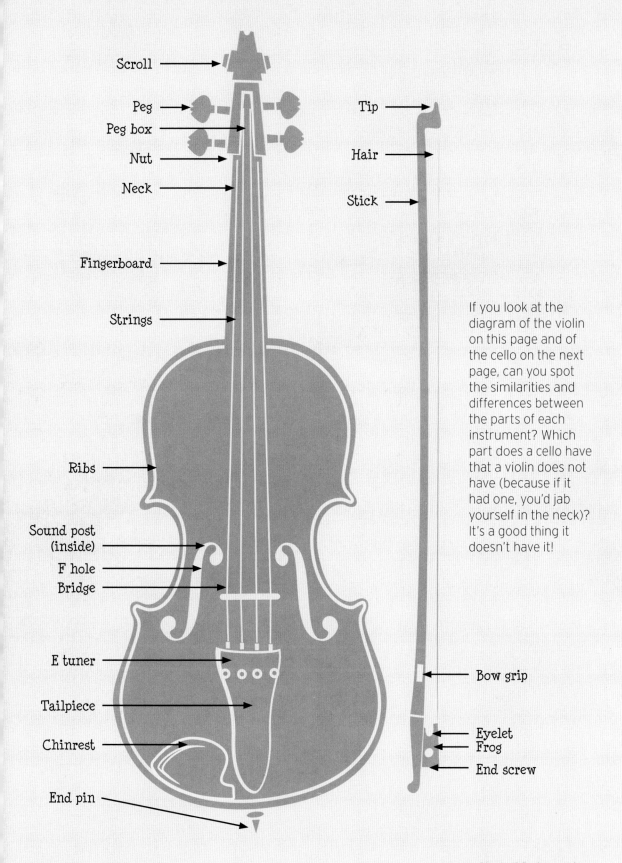

Scroll

Peg

Peg box

Nut

Neck

Fingerboard

Strings

Ribs

Sound post (inside)

F hole

Bridge

E tuner

Tailpiece

Chinrest

End pin

Tip

Hair

Stick

If you look at the diagram of the violin on this page and of the cello on the next page, can you spot the similarities and differences between the parts of each instrument? Which part does a cello have that a violin does not have (because if it had one, you'd jab yourself in the neck)? It's a good thing it doesn't have it!

Bow grip

Eyelet

Frog

End screw

Viola

The viola is like the big brother of the violin, and it fills the gap between the high-sounding violin and the low-sounding cello. It has a really mellow sound. It has four strings just like the violin, but they sound at different note pitches:

C G D A   (from low to high)

So the viola is the middle-sounding stringed instrument, and it often plays harmonies or accompaniments. Violas are vital members of every orchestra and string ensemble, but they don't get as many chances to shine as the violin. However, there are a few beautiful solos for the viola.

Most viola players or **violists** start on the violin, or a violin with the letter strings of a viola. This is because a viola is bigger than a violin and you need to be big and strong enough to hold it up to play it. You also need to place your fingers further apart to make the notes. All violins are the same size, but violas come in sizes based on the number of inches wide they are.

Can you think of a rhyme to remember these 'letter strings'?

The viola's lowest note is the C below middle C, which is well below the bottom of the treble clef. However, it is nearly in the middle of the bass clef, so it leaves lots of lines and spaces in the bass clef stave, below that low C, which the viola can't ever use! That low C is only just off the bottom of alto clef. Remember, stringed instruments don't transpose, so the alto clef fits the viola's notes perfectly. Sometimes they go into the treble clef when they play very high, but not often!

Cello

The cello looks like a big violin and shares all the same features, but it is actually a very different instrument. The cello player, called a **cellist**, holds the big body of the cello between her knees and rests it against her chest. She holds her left arm up to reach the strings on the fingerboard, pressing them to form the notes, and moves the bow from left to right with her right hand to make the sound.

Because a cello is held flat against the cellist's body, rather than sticking out like a violin or viola, the cellist has to hold her bow in a different way. However, she still moves it to the left and right at different angles across the strings to produce a sound in exactly the same way. Have a look at the diagram below and compare and contrast it with the violin on the previous page.

Remember me? I'm Alisha Alto. Violas are special because they are the only common musical instrument to read music off me all the time. In fact, the alto clef is sometimes called the viola clef!

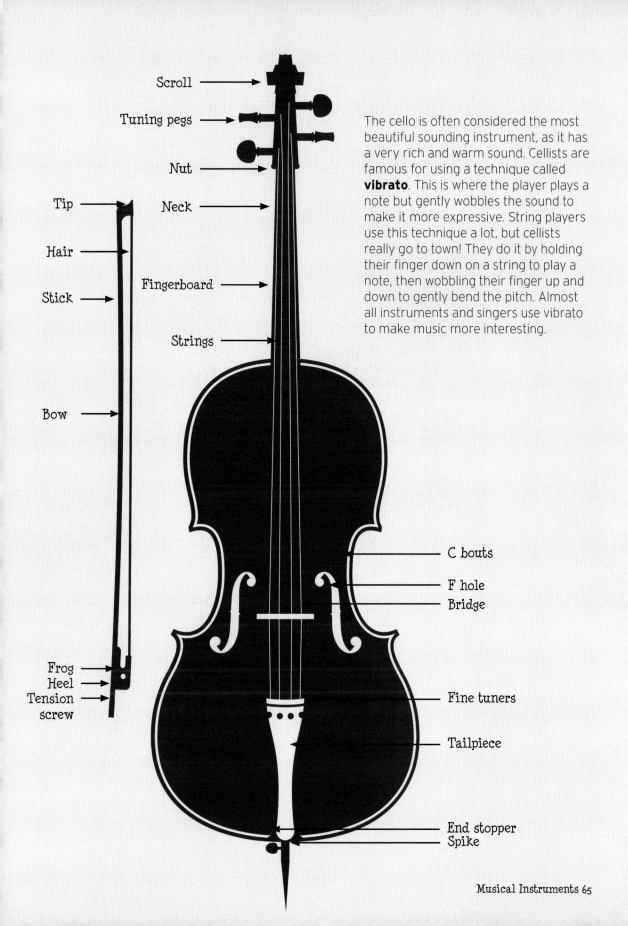

Scroll

Tuning pegs

Nut

Tip

Neck

Hair

Stick

Fingerboard

Bow

Strings

The cello is often considered the most beautiful sounding instrument, as it has a very rich and warm sound. Cellists are famous for using a technique called **vibrato**. This is where the player plays a note but gently wobbles the sound to make it more expressive. String players use this technique a lot, but cellists really go to town! They do it by holding their finger down on a string to play a note, then wobbling their finger up and down to gently bend the pitch. Almost all instruments and singers use vibrato to make music more interesting.

C bouts

F hole

Bridge

Frog
Heel
Tension
screw

Fine tuners

Tailpiece

End stopper
Spike

Double bass

The double bass is not from exactly the same family as the violin, viola and cello. It is actually a member of the viol family. It has a slightly more sloping shape and the pattern of strings is different, too. The violin, viola and cello follow a pattern of having a count of five steps between their strings:

	Bottom String	Steps	2nd String	Steps	3rd String	Steps	Top String
Violin	G	+5	D	+5	A	+5	E
Viola	C	+5	G	+5	D	+5	A
Cello	C	+5	G	+5	D	+5	A
Dounble Bass	E	+4	A	+4	D	+4	G

Remember when we spoke about the steps between notes in chapter 1? We call these steps **intervals**. The bottom string on a violin is a G and the second string is a D. This is a gap of 5 steps, and therefore an interval of a 5th. All the strings go up in intervals of a 5th. However, the gap between the strings on a double bass (and a bass guitar) are gaps of four steps and therefore an interval of a 4th. But the double bass has a count of four steps between strings. Some **bassists** like to have an extra string, another four steps higher (C), to give them more high notes.

A double bass is played the same way as a cello, only the bassist has to stand or sit on a high stool as the instrument is too big to fit between his knees!

Next to the tuba, the double bass is the deepest sounding instrument of the orchestra and string orchestra. It is also the only orchestral instrument that regularly crosses over into popular music. You can hear it in most jazz bands and in a lot of popular or musical theatre bands, too. This is because it is good for playing funky tunes at a low pitch that don't work so well on woodwind and brass instruments.

Double basses (and all stringed instruments) can make a short pinging sound if the player uses his finger to pluck the string, rather than scraping the bow across it. This technique is called **pizzicato**. The player hooks his finger over the string then uses the pad of the finger to pull against the string, making a twanging sound. Because the double bass is so huge and the strings are really thick, they vibrate really loudly when plucked. If they are pulled hard enough, they will slap back against the fingerboard, and this style of playing is known as slap bass.

Electric bass

The electric bass is like a double bass, but it needs to be plugged into an amplifier (or amp) to produce sound. The amplifier makes it very loud and can change the tonal quality of the notes, too. Tiny metal disks, called pickups, sense the vibrations as the musician plays and turn them into an electric wave, which is then fed through the amplifier.

Because an electric bass is smaller than a double bass, the player can hold it sideways and rest the weight on a strap, which goes over her shoulder. It has four strings like a double bass: E, A, D and G, and many players like to have a fifth string too, for extra notes.

The electric bass has become really useful in pop and rock music, modern classical music, show music, and music for film and TV, because it is so much smaller than the double bass.

Harp

Harps are another instrument that has been around since ancient times and they have a rippling, quite mysterious sound. The harp plays music off both a treble and a bass stave. That is because the harpist can play notes with her left hand and right hand at the same time. They have a wide range of notes, from low to high, because of the huge number of strings.

Harps are very big, with a curvy shape, so the strings go from very long to very short. The longer the string, the lower the note that can be played. A harpist plucks all the notes with her fingers. She generally uses her left hand for the low notes and her right hand for the high notes. A harp also has pedals, which loosen and tighten the strings to make sharp and flat notes.

Guitar

The guitar is often thought of as a modern instrument, made famous by rock music. That is true of electric guitars, but acoustic guitars have been around for hundreds of years. Guitars are very popular partly because of their long history, but they are also relatively cheap and easy to learn, and are very good at accompanying other instruments and singers.

The electric guitar is well known in popular music, but it is used a lot in theatre shows, too. Because it is electric, its sound can be made louder with an amplifier, and by using distortion pedals you can change the sound.

An acoustic guitar does not need to be plugged in to work! Like orchestral stringed instruments (violin, cello etc.), acoustic guitars have a big, wooden, hollow body that allows the sound to echo and reverberate.

Both types of guitar work in exactly the same way. They have six strings and the sound is made by plucking a single string at a time or by strumming all the strings together. Because you can play all the strings at once on the guitar, it is very easy to play chords. The strings are:

E A D G B E

Notice how they don't follow an exact pattern of fours or fives like the other stringed instruments (see page 60). Like all the stringed instruments, when you press your finger down, the note of that string gets higher by a half-step. However, guitars (and bass guitars) have frets, which are the little horizontal metal lines underneath the strings on the fretboard. These tell the player exactly where to put his finger to make a note of a set number of steps.

To find out more about the guitar and have a go at playing some tunes on it, go to page 107.

Percussion

There are hundreds and hundreds of different percussion instruments and some composers and **percussionists** use found objects, such as bins and colanders, to make sounds with in their music. Percussion instruments are hit or scraped with the hands or **mallets** and **beaters** (special sticks with rounded heads made out of various materials) to produce sounds.

Unpitched percussion

Perhaps the most famous percussion instruments are drums. There are many different types, with different traditions and ways of being played. The term '**unpitched percussion**' means you can't play tunes on these instruments, as they don't have the ability to play different notes.

Most people learn drums by practising on a drum kit. A drum kit is made up of a collection of drums and cymbals (metal discs, which sound rather like a gong).

You need good **coordination** to play a drum kit, as you could be using your feet and both hands to do different things, but in time with each other! All of these drums may also be used separately in orchestras and bands. They are used to add drama and highlight certain bits of the music. They also can be used to picture a scene, making thunder sounds or gunshot sounds for example. The drums include:

Bass drum The biggest, lowest and most booming drum. It is played with a giant fluffy beater, or hit with a foot pedal when in a drum kit.

Snare drum This makes a rattling sound. It is used for military marches and can make a rolling sound. It is played with drumsticks.

Suspended cymbal This sits on a pole and is hit, scraped or rolled to make different metallic sounds.

Hi hat A pair of cymbals that smash together when a foot pedal is pressed. The cymbals can also be tapped and scraped by drumsticks and beaters to make lots of different sounds and beats.

Other unpitched percussion instruments are:

Triangle This is just a metal bar bent into the shape of a triangle, which is tapped with a special metal beater to make a tingly, pinging, metallic sound.

Clash cymbals These are big cymbals that you hold with straps and bash together.

Tambourine A small round or semicircular bar that has cut-out areas filled with lots of little metal discs, like tiny cymbals. Some tambourines have a skin stretched across the top, like a drum. It makes a shimmery sound when you shake it. You probably have some at your school; they are easy to play and good for making rhythms.

Tam tam This giant bronze gong hangs from a special rack. It is hit with a giant fluffy beater to make a huge rumbling, shimmering sound.

Now for some different types of drums, cymbals and shakers from around the world! These are samba instruments, from the traditional and **fusion** music of South America and Latin American culture. They are used a lot in modern music in the West, especially pop music:

Bongos Little hand-held drums that come in a pair joined together. One drum is taller than the other. You hold bongos between your knees and tap them with the palm of your hands.

Congas Giant, tall bongos with a deep sound.

Guiro A cone or tube with ridges on that you scrape with a wooden stick to make a croaky, scratchy noise.

Cowbell A metal bell in the shape of a cone, which you hit with a beater to make a loud ringing sound.

Maracas Shakers with big round heads and sticks for handles.

Claves Wooden sticks that are clapped together to make a clicking sound.

Drums from other parts of the world include:

Djembe This is a popular traditional drum from Africa. You may have seen one in your school. It has a distinctive, egg-timer shape and often comes in bright colours. You hit it with your hands, and there are different techniques for doing this.

Cabassa This shaker from Africa has metal beads wrapped around a central cylinder. You hold the beads in one hand and use the handle to twizzle it so the beads scrape across the cylinder.

Cajon Say 'Kah-hon'. This is another African drum, widely used in the Middle East too. It is now one of the most popular alternatives to the drum kit across the world. It is basically just a big wooden box: the percussionist sits on top of it and taps, slaps and hits the edges to make different sounds and beats. It has a hole in the back to let the sound echo out and an extra layer of thin wood, or sometimes chains, across one side to made a rattling sound.

Dhol This popular traditional drum from India has a skin on both ends of the drum, so you can play a different rhythm on each end at the same time. The drum is held on a strap that goes over the shoulder. You hit the drum with special wooden sticks and players (dholis) often dance and make special movements with their face while they play.

Tabla An Indian drum played with the hands in many different ways to produce really complicated beats and sounds. Good tabla players use a series of finger taps, hits and slaps to create intricate rhythms.

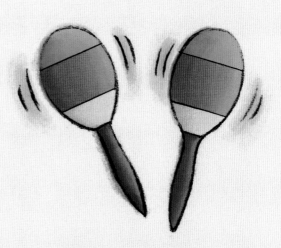

Pitched percussion

Pitched percussion instruments are those that have lots of little keys, all set to a different note pitch, so it is possible to play tunes. The keys are made of large wooden or metal bars. Here are some common examples:

Xylophone The xylophone is a big instrument made up of different wooden bars tuned to notes. It is played with mallets, usually with one in each hand, so the percussionist can move between notes quickly. Good players may use two in each hand to make chords in the music.

Glockenspiel The glockenspiel is smaller than a xylophone, with metal bars that sound quite high when tunes are played on them. When it is used in marching and military bands, the percussionist straps it to his chest and plays sideways! The metal bars are played with little beaters.

Vibraphone A vibraphone looks a bit like a xylophone or glockenspiel, but each metal bar is paired with a tube beneath it. Inside the tubes are little wafting paddles to create a vibrato sound: this is where the name of the instrument comes from! The paddles are run by a motor and controlled by a foot pedal. This means the vibraphone has to be plugged into mains electricity to work.

Marimbas The marimba is very much like the xylophone but it is bigger and generally has more wooden bars to create notes, especially deep notes. Marimba players often play piano music, using mallets to hit the bars rather than using their fingers on the keys of a piano. Marimbas also sound quite unique - woody and echoing - thanks to the giant resonator tubes underneath the bars, which make the sound louder and more booming.

Tubular bells These big 'bells' are actually long metal tubes! They are lined up in order of size, to make the pitch of different notes. The player hits them with big wooden hammers and they can be heard over the whole orchestra or band, pealing out a tune.

Timpani These are sometimes called kettledrums. They are huge, metal-bottomed drums, which come in sets. Each drum can only play one note, but you can play tunes across a set of three, four or sometimes five different-sized drums. The modern ones are also fitted with foot pedals that allow the percussionist or **timpanist** to change the note of that drum in the middle of a piece. They are hit with beaters and most players have a selection of hard and soft beaters to make different sounds. They can be very loud and one drum can be heard across the entire orchestra or band!

Keys

Piano

Most musicians learn the piano at some point, because it helps us practise the theory we learnt about in Chapter 1. Pianos have a very recognizable pattern of white and black wooden keys. High notes are played by the right hand and low notes by the left hand. The piano player, called a **pianist**, reads music off two staves at once. The right hand follows the treble clef and the left hand follows the bass clef. In Chapter 5, you can have a go at learning the piano.

A piano is a great instrument because you can play lots of notes at once. This means you can play tunes and accompaniments at the same time. Or, two people can play the same piano at the same time, so you can play duets.

The piano is an odd instrument. It counts partly as a percussion instrument because you strike the keys with your fingers (though you don't hit them). If you ever get the chance, ask someone to open the lid on his or her piano so you can look inside. You will see that it is full of strings, just like a harp! However, instead of the strings being plucked, they are hit by little fluffy hammers that are attached to each key.

Pianos also have a set of pedals, which can make the sound quieter, or hold certain notes, or makes the notes smooth into each other. This last one, called the **damper pedal**, is the most popular and means that many notes can be heard at once.

The word 'piano' comes from an earlier version of the modern piano, called the pianoforte. 'Pianoforte' literally means 'quiet-loud'. Pianofortes were the first keyboard instruments that could play dynamics – they could play loudly and quietly. (This is still true on a modern-day piano: if you press a key softly, the note that comes out is quiet, whereas if you strike the key hard, the note sounds loud.) Before the pianoforte, the main keyboard instrument was the harpsichord, which had little hooks to pluck the strings, and sounded a bit like a harp, but could only play at one volume.

To find out more about how you play the piano (or keyboard), turn to page 101.

Keyboard and synthesizer

Keyboards are just electric pianos, though they can be programmed with many different types of sounds. You may have practised using a keyboard at school to make drum sounds on one of its special settings. Synthesizers take this one step further by allowing you to create sounds electronically.

Synthesizers have a keyboard-like set of keys, so you can play a melody into the computer and then the computer's software manipulates the sounds. Anything that can be recorded digitally can be **sampled** into a computer, even crazy sounds like car horns or drills. The computer then turns them into specific notes, which are played on the synthesizer.

Organ

The organ is the biggest musical instrument in the world. It has keys just like a piano, but instead of strings it has huge pipes. Bellows inside the organ push air through the pipes. This gives the organ a big, booming sound, especially on the low notes.

The organ is different to the piano because as well as having keys for your fingers and pedals to change the tone and dampen the organ, it also has a whole row of giant keys to be played by the organist's feet! The organist slides up and down the seat to play tunes on these foot keys, which operate the largest of the bellows. Because of this, music for the organ doesn't just have two lines of music - one for each hand - but an extra line at the bottom for the foot pedal notes.

As well as the extra rows of keys and foot pedals, the organ also has a lot of buttons, known as **stops**. These affect the movement of air in the pipes, which changes the sounds produced.

Many churches and synagogues have an organ to be played as part of the worship service. The organist may play arrangements of hymns and psalms for the congregation to listen to, or for people to sing. There are also special pieces for ceremonies, such as weddings, funerals and festivals like Passover and Easter. That tradition continues today, though in recent times electric organs have been increasingly used, as they are smaller and cheaper.

Electric organs have been used in pop and rock music. In the USA it is also traditional to hear folk and popular songs played on the organ in the intervals at basketball, baseball and hockey matches.

Giant organs

The largest organ in the world, and largest musical instrument ever built, is in Boardwalk Hall, Atlantic City, New Jersey, USA. It has a massive 33,114 pipes (this is the official count, as no one is totally sure!) and fills a hall bigger than 155,742 cubic metres (5.5 million cubic feet). Unfortunately, it got damaged in a hurricane in 1944 and wasn't properly restored until 2003, when the Historic Organ Restoration Committee got the money to do it. It is so big that the restoration is still going on! However, you can visit the hall and be shown around the organ, as well as hear it in free concerts at certain times.

Accordion

The accordion is a strange-looking instrument with piano-like keys, which is held sideways and pumped by bellows. The bellows are powered by the accordion player's hand as he pushes the body of the accordion in and out. Because of this squeezing action, the instrument is sometimes called a squeezebox. There are little stop keys on the squeezing side of the accordion, opposite the side with the keys. These are not used to change the sound, but to fill in the accompaniments and chords under the tune.

The accordion is found all over the world and is used a lot in traditional folk music (see Chapter 4). It is the traditional instrument of Bosnia and Herzegovina and people all over Eastern Europe love its sound. It can also be found in the popular music of South America and is even enjoying a comeback in Western classical music, appearing as a solo instrument in Western Europe and South East Asia.

Voice

The voice is probably the best instrument to make music with, as we all have one! Have you ever stopped to wonder how many different ways you can make music with your voice? As well as singing (and there are loads of different ways of singing), we can use our voices to rap, chant, shriek, shout, squeal, whisper and whistle.

Everyone's voice is unique. However, people's voices can be roughly divided into groups based on how they sound, and how high or low they are. For example, men and women have different voices and boys and girls have different voices. When boys and girls hit puberty, their voices change suddenly and become adult voices. This is more noticeable when it happens to boys and their voice is described as 'breaking'. It sounds scary, but it is normal and most boys get used to singing with their new voice. In time, many become even better singers. Generally, our voices get gradually lower as we get older.

Remember when we learnt about the different clefs, and how each one is used for high instruments and low instruments? Different types of voice are named after the clefs, depending on how high or low they are. The main types are: soprano, mezzo soprano and alto for ladies and tenor, baritone and bass for the men.

Try all of these voice sounds. How do they sound? Can you think of any more? Some of these voice sounds do not sound so nice! Which ones would you want to use in a piece about ghosts and monsters?

Hang on a second! Why isn't there a voice named after me? It says here the highest voice is soprano. What about a treble?

Calm down, Trudi! There is a voice named after you, but treble is the highest voice ever and these types are the most common voices.

Oh. So a treble singer is much rarer than a bass singer?

Yes, though a treble singer could turn into a bass singer!

Wow! How does that work?

Well, we often use the word treble to describe the very high and pipe-like sound of children's voices, particularly boys. People often describe the sound as angelic. But boys don't stay trebles forever as their voices will break and they will become a bass, baritone or tenor, which is obviously the best!

However high or low someone's voice is, they can train it for different styles of music. Each type of music requires a slightly different way of using the voice. You can learn more about these in Chapter 5.

Now that we've learnt about all the types of instruments and voices, I wonder what they sound like when played together?

Yes, I can't wait to find out where we can play and sing together with our friends!

3
MUSICAL ENSEMBLES

So we now know about lots of different musical instruments, but how do they work together and sound together? It is good to practise an instrument on your own, but it's a lot more fun when you get together with other people to make music. You can make any groups you like with your friends, but when you are good players, you could join a youth or community ensemble. Here are some common ensembles.

Large ensembles

The orchestra

The orchestra (or symphony orchestra; sometimes just called a symphony) is probably the first thing people think of when they think of a big group of instruments. It is made up of the four main families of instruments: strings, woodwind, brass and percussion.

A **conductor** stands in front of the orchestra and makes signals to show the musicians when and in what style to play the music. She moves her hands or a special little stick called a **baton** to do this. Conductors are musicians who have a talent for pulling the best moods and colours out of the music, and also for telling the musicians what needs to be rehearsed. They will have started by learning to play an instrument or even a few instruments, but have decided that they want to be in charge!

Being an orchestral musician can be a job and this is how the players in all the big symphony orchestras earn a living. Most will have studied their instrument at **conservatoire** (special music college) or university and spend hours each day preparing and practising, so they are the best. This makes them **professional** musicians. Of course, there are school and community orchestras too, for people still learning and playing for fun!

There are many different instruments in an orchestra and different numbers of players of each instrument. For example, there are often at least 20 violins sometimes more, whereas there are only a few pieces ever written that need more than one tuba or piccolo! As such there are different parts of music written for each instrument, so the music is more interesting. The bowed strings are split into 5 parts – two violin parts, known as first and second violins, violas, cellos and basses, who normally play exactly the same part within their section. The woodwind, brass and percussion tend to have a part each e.g. 1st flute, 2nd flute and piccolo. First parts generally have all the solos and more of the tunes and higher notes, whilst the second parts provide harmony. This is true for all our ensembles.

Orchestras have changed and evolved a lot over hundreds and hundreds of years (see Chapter 4), but a modern symphony orchestra is normally arranged like this:

Typical instruments in a symphony orchestra	20 violins (10 first violins, 10 second violins), 8 violas, 8 cellos, 8 double basses, 1 piano, 2 harps, 1 piccolo, 2 flutes, 2 oboes, cor anglais, 3 clarinets (combination of E♭, B♭, A and bass), 2 bassoons, 1 contrabassoon, 4 French horns, 3 trumpets, 3 trombones (2 tenor, 1 bass), 1 tuba, 1 timpani, 3 percussion/drums. Conductor. Occasionally a saxophone or euphonium.

Famous works for this ensemble

- Ludwig van Beethoven, Symphony No. 5 (Beethoven wrote nine symphonies and they're all good!).
- Pyotr Tchaikovsky, *1812 Overture* (Tchaikovsky also wrote six symphonies).
- Giuseppe Verdi, *Aida* (Prelude).
- John Williams, *Star Wars* (music from the film).
- Maurice Ravel, *Bolero*.
- Gioachino Rossini, *The Thieving Magpie* (Overture).
- Gustav Holst, *The Planets*.

Examples of this type of ensemble

London Symphony Orchestra (UK); Vienna Philharmonic (Austria); Berlin Philharmonic Orchestra, Leipzig Gewandhaus Orchestra (Germany); New York Philharmonic, Cleveland Orchestra (USA); Israel Philharmonic Orchestra (Israel); Melbourne Symphony Orchestra (Australia).

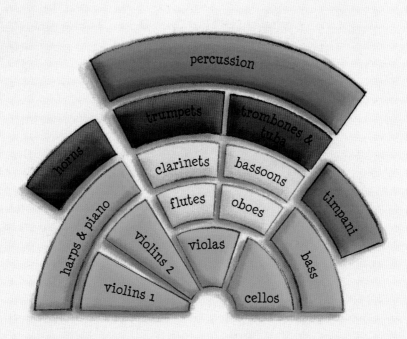

The wind orchestra

The wind orchestra is sometimes known as a wind band or symphonic wind ensemble. It is like an orchestra, but does not have a string section. However, there is usually a double bass and/or a bass guitar, as well as some other instruments from the wind and brass families that aren't normally in an orchestra - such as the saxophone and euphonium. This is a good place for woodwind players to get practice playing their subsidiary instruments, as lots of different types of clarinet, flute and saxophone are used as well as the contrabassoon and cor anglais.

There are only a few professional wind bands. Most wind bands are made up of **amateur musicians**. Amateur musicians are often very good players, but they don't have to make their living out of music or put all of their energy into it. They do not practise as much, and their main income comes from their day job, such as being a doctor or a bus driver. The only professional or semi-professional musician in a wind band is the conductor, who gets paid to lead the band, although sometimes he will 'buy' professional players to play hard parts or teach the instrumentalists how to play their part. Some wind bands are part of the armed forces of a country, so they are professional; all armed forces musicians are trained soldiers too!

The wind orchestra typically looks like this:

| Typical instruments in a wind orchestra | 1 piccolo, 4 flutes (2 first flute, 2 second flute), 2 oboes, 1 cor anglais, 1 E♭ clarinet, 6 clarinets (2 first clarinet, 2 second clarinet, 2 third clarinet), 1 bass clarinet, 4 saxophones (2 alto, 1 tenor, 1 baritone), 2 bassoons, 1 contrabassoon, 4 French horns, 3 trumpets, 3 trombones (2 tenor, 1 bass), 2 euphoniums/baritones, 2 tubas, 1 double bass/bass guitar, drums, percussion. Conductor. |

Famous works for this ensemble

- Percy Grainger, *Lincolnshire Posy*.
- Gustav Holst, *First Suite in E♭ Major for Military Band*.
- John P. Sousa, The *Stars and Stripes Forever*.
- Kenneth Hesketh, *Masque*.
- Guy Woolfenden, *Gallimaufry*.
- Eric Whitacre, *Cloudburst*.

Examples of this type of ensemble

Professional: Dallas Wind Symphony (USA); Osaka Municipal Symphonic Band, Tokyo Kosei Wind Orchestra (Japan).
Military: United States Marine Band (USA); Band of the Grenadier Guards (UK).
Community (amateur): Salt Lake Symphonic Winds (USA); Birmingham Symphonic Winds (UK).

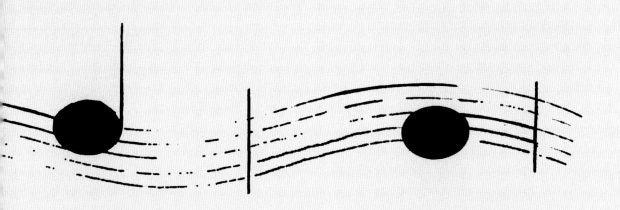

The string orchestra

The string orchestra is made up of lots of instruments solely from the strings family. Sometimes it has a conductor and sometimes it is led by the **leader**, who is a player of the first violin (which plays the top line) and sits at the very front. There are often auditions for the job, so it is usually the best or most experienced violinist who gets the job of leader. He or she shows people when to come in by using their bow and movements of their head and arms. All the other violins follow their movements.

It is sometimes hard to tell which music was written for a string orchestra and which was written for **string quartet**, where only one player plays each part. This is because most composers, especially hundreds of years ago, didn't write exact instructions on the music.

Typical instruments in a string orchestra

16 violins (8 first violins, 8 second violins), 6 violas, 6 cellos, 4 double basses. Sometimes with harps.

Famous works for this ensemble

- Wolfgang Amadeus Mozart, *Eine kleine Nachtmusik* (one of the most famous pieces in the world!).
- Samuel Barber, *Adagio for Strings*.
- Béla Bartók, *Divertimento for String Orchestra*.
- Benjamin Britten, *Simple Symphony*.

Examples of this type of ensemble

Most string orchestras perform as a section taken from the main symphony orchestra (e.g. the strings of the Chicago Symphony), or as a session orchestra where players - who may not have met before - turn up for one set of rehearsals and a concert. Most counties and states have a youth or training string orchestra.

The jazz band

Most jazz bands are led by the rhythm section, so they do not need a conductor. This means the piano or drums often counts people in and gives cues, like the leader in the string orchestra. The jazz band is based on saxophones and brass. Together the wind instruments are known as 'horns', even though none of these instruments is a horn! People tend to have special jazz instruments too. You'd use a different trumpet in an orchestra to a jazz band.

Often, jazz bands are professional groups, although of course people also set up jazz bands for fun. Most jazz groups have to **promote** their music themselves and find their own concerts and **gigs**. They often play for clubs and bars and festivals, as well as recording their music. A jazz musician is often self-employed, which means he or she has to find their own work to get money to live on, rather than being employed by a single company. Many jazz musicians are in lots of different bands and often work at other jobs too, such as teaching their instrument or working in a studio. This is called being a **freelancer**. Lots of classical instrumentalists and singers do this too!

Jazz bands are a bit more relaxed in their set-up than other ensembles. Mostly, the musicians stand to play, though sometimes the front row of saxophone players sits down. Some bands have flutes, tubas, clarinets and French horns in them too. However, the standard set-up is like this:

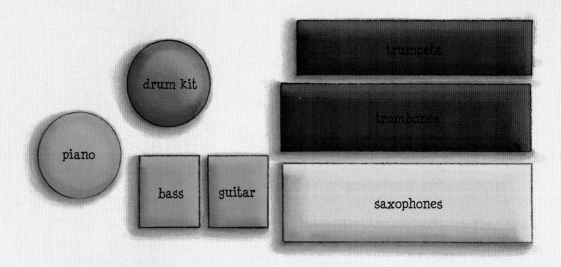

Typical instruments in a jazz band	5 saxophones (2 alto, 2 tenor, 1 baritone), 4 trumpets/flugelhorns, 4 trombones (3 tenor, 1 bass), double bass/bass guitar, guitar, drums, piano. Sometimes with a vocalist.
Famous works for this ensemble	• Glenn Miller, *In the Mood*. • Benny Goodman, *Sing Sing Sing*. • Pee Wee Ellis/Jaco Pastorius, *The Chicken*. • Dave Brubeck, *Take Five*.
Examples of this type of ensemble	Count Basie Orchestra, Glenn Miller Orchestra (USA); BBC Big Band (UK); Berlin Contemporary Jazz Orchestra (Germany); Danish Radio Big Band (Denmark).

The brass band

The brass band as we know it today is a tradition that comes from Britain, but brass bands are becoming more common in places such as Scandinavia, Australia, New Zealand, Canada and the USA. People in Japan, Taiwan and China are beginning to learn brass band instruments, too.

In the UK, the first brass bands started when mineworkers met up after work to play music and relax. The mining company would sponsor the players and provide the instruments, and there were many social events for the band and their families. Brass bands compete with each other through world rankings, just like in all the major sports leagues. The bands go to events where they play a set piece of music known as the test piece, and get points for how accurately and musically they perform it.

Brass bands are made up of instruments from just one family: the brass. Because the instruments have similar tones, the overall sound of a brass band is very rich and mellow, and blends together really well. Many people compare this to the way that voices in a choir blend together. Brass bands have strong links to church and gospel music. Most study hymns to practise playing together as a band, and some churches even have a resident brass band to play in Sunday morning worship.

The brass band typically looks like this:

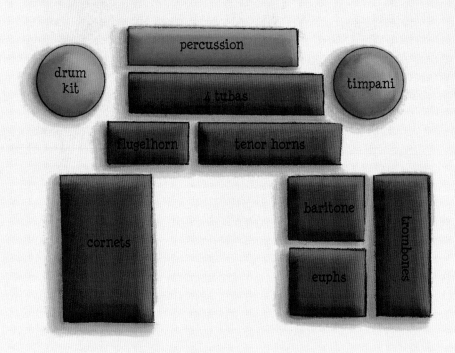

| Typical instruments in a brass band | 1 soprano cornet, 9 cornets (solo cornet, **repiano cornet**, second cornet, and third cornet), 1 flugelhorn, 3 tenor horns, 2 baritone horns, 2 euphoniums, 3 trombones (2 tenor, 1 bass), 4 tubas (2 B♭, 2 E♭), 3 percussionists. |

| Famous works for this ensemble | • Gilbert Vinter, *Spectrum*.
• Eric Ball, *Resurgam*.
• Philip Wilby, *Paganini Variations*.
• Philip Sparke, *Tallis Variations*. |

| Examples of this type of ensemble | Black Dyke Band, Grimethorpe Colliery Band, Brighouse and Rastrick Brass Band, Cory Band, (UK); Brass Band Bürgermusik Luzern (Switzerland); Fountain City Brass Band (USA); Brass Band Schoonhoven (Netherlands); Eikanger-Bjørsvik Band (Norway). |

The choir

The choir or chorus is a big ensemble for singers! The different types of voices make the different tonal sounds instead of instruments, and each part in the choir has its own tune to sing. Sometimes all parts of the choir will all sing exactly the same thing, in a **homophonic texture**. At other times there will be three or four different parts per voice part, so there are many tunes and harmonies happening at once. Some choirs are just made up of ladies' voices, which sound high; male voice choirs only have men's voices, which sound low.

Because the ensemble is made up entirely of voices, the sound blends together really well.

In fact, when you sing in a choir, you sing in a different way to when you are singing a solo, and try to blend in and match the sounds and words of the people around you.

Often choirs sing alone but they can also sing with orchestras in a huge combined ensemble. The choir can also sing to back up solo singers, often with a band or orchestra in a musical theatre or opera (see below). In the table opposite we are examining traditional classical choirs, but groups of singers can sing anything and often choirs sing lots of cool voice only versions of chart and show songs.

Operas and musical theatre shows are plays with singing, where the chorus takes on the role of telling the story, and backing the soloists who play the main characters. Operas tend to be in the Western classical style with some of the most popular ones, such as *La bohème* or *The Magic Flute* being hundreds of years old! They are often sung in the language of their composers' country so people need the words on a big screen to know what's going on! Musicals are more modern in style and use elements of jazz and pop music. They are almost always sung in English. Some famous examples are *Wicked* and *Phantom of the Opera*. Both of these types of show have live musicians in an orchestra or band, great solo singers and choirs, as well as colourful costumes!

Typical voices in a choir	Sopranos, altos, tenors and basses (SATB). Female choirs typically: soprano 1, soprano 2, alto (SSA). Male voice choir typically: tenor 1, tenor 2, baritone, bass (TTBB).
Famous works for this ensemble	· Johann Sebastian Bach, *Mass in B minor*. · George Frideric Handel, *Messiah*. · Carl Orff, *Carmina Burana*. · John Rutter, *Gloria*. · Karl Jenkins, *Adiemus*.
Examples of this type of ensemble	The Sixteen, the Monteverdi Choir (UK); Chanticleer (USA); RIAS Kammerchor (Germany); Swedish Radio Choir (Sweden); Chœur de Chambre Accentus (France).

These are all just suggestions of groups and pieces to listen too, to get you started. Why not make a mind map of the pieces you listen to, and then the ensembles and pieces you found through them?

Try looking for music by the same composer or look for other recordings by the same ensemble. Keep a listening journal to save the ones you like the best.

Small ensembles

Small ensembles are groups of less than ten musicians. Often they will only have one musician per instrument or part. We call this music that is played or sung by a small group of people **chamber music**.

Quartets and quintets

A solo is one instrument playing alone, a duo is two instruments playing together, and a trio is three instruments together. Quartets are simply four instruments (or voices) together and quintets are five instruments or voices. Any combination of instruments is fine, but here are some typical sets of instruments, that lots of composers have written music for.

Jazz also follows this tradition, so a jazz quartet could include any combination of instruments from a jazz band. Some famous examples include Louis Armstrong and His Hot Five and The Dave Brubeck Quartet.

Type of ensemble		Name of ensemble	Instruments
Quartet	**String**	String quartet	2 violins, viola and cello
	Wind	Wind quartet	Flute, clarinet, oboe, bassoon
	Brass	Brass quartet	2 tubas, 2 euphoniums
	Vocal	Barbershop quartet (usually male, though female versions exist)	Lead, tenor, baritone, bass (male barbershop)
Quintet	**Strings & piano**	Piano quintet	2 violins, viola, cello and piano
	Wind	Wind quintet	Flute, clarinet, oboe, bassoon and French horn
	Brass	Brass quintet	2 trumpets, French horn, trombone, tuba
		Brass band quintet	2 cornets, tenor horn, euphonium, tuba

Chamber music with friends

Which groups can you make with your friends? Can you make a musical quartet or quintet? Can you make any on the list above? If you don't have instruments, borrow some from your school. If you need to, draft in a teacher or parent to play with you or sing!

See if you can find some music for your ensemble. Do some research into the songs written for this type of ensemble and even if they're too hard to play, listen to them.

Ah, a piano quintet! That will have five pianos in it, won't it?

Sorry, Barry, but no! Because a piano is so large and only needs one player to play lots of harmonies, it is added to four other instruments, often a string quartet, to make a chamber group.

Now I come to think of it, I don't think I could fit five pianos into my lounge!

Rock or pop band

Pop and rock bands count as small ensembles as there are rarely more than six people in one band. However there are large groups of popular musicians or fusion musicians (musicians who play folk and world music but in a popular style), known as collectives.

Pop bands are more likely to be groups of singers who perform to backing tracks, whilst rock bands more commonly have just the one singer but lots of instruments, including guitars.

Typical instruments	Vocalist, 2 guitars (lead and rhythm), bass guitar, drums, keyboard/synthesizer. Sometimes with 'horns' e.g. trumpet, saxophone, trombone.
Some famous examples of this type of ensemble	The Beatles, The Rolling Stones, Coldplay, Fall Out Boy, Maroon 5, Genesis, The Killers, the Bee Gees.

Itching to join your local ensemble, or start one with your friends? Let's look at how to play some of the most popular instruments!

4
LEARN TO PLAY

In this chapter we are going to make music on some popular instruments. You will learn the first notes and try some tunes. If you find that you like playing an instrument and can do all of the exercises here, or want to try another instrument such as a violin or clarinet, talk to your teacher and parents about getting lessons. It could be the start of a really exciting adventure and a lifetime of fun. Enjoy making music!

Recorder

Let's get playing! Suck on your finger as though you were licking some chocolate sauce off it. This is how your lips should be when you put the recorder in your mouth - relaxed and floppy. Make sure you seal your lips all the way around the top of the recorder so that air cannot come out the sides of your mouth but goes straight down into the recorder tube. The line of holes should be facing straight up to the ceiling. The curved bit of the top of the recorder should be facing your chin.

Now you can start to blow. It is very important to start gently and slowly. Imagine you are blowing down a long straw. You can practise the proper way to blow by using a finger: hold it up in front of you like you're making a 'shushing' sound and blow on the tip. Is the air constant, warm and gentle?

Super! Blow into the recorder in the same way and it will make a nice sound. The holes on top of the recorder are called finger holes and if you look on the back of it, there is one lonely hole called the thumbhole. Using your left hand, put your left thumb on that hole. Bring your index finger (first finger) round the recorder and put it on the first hole at the top of the recorder. Keeping your fingers in this position, blow into the recorder. Well done! You have learnt your first note: it is a B note. A recorder is a high instrument, so it uses the treble clef.

Can you remember what a B looks like in treble clef?

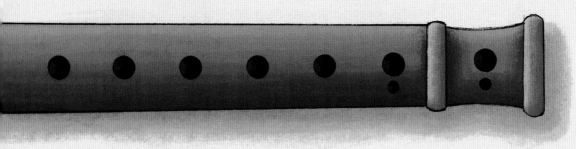

Play a few Bs. Try not to blow too hard or the recorder will squeak; we are aiming for a beautiful, clear tone.

Once you can play a long B note, without squeaking and with relaxed lips, try playing lots of short, separate B notes. Do this by using your tongue to make a 'too' sound on the end of the recorder, behind your teeth.

Try playing a string of one-beat notes with your B finger and thumb. Say 'too-too-too-too'.

TOP TIP!
Remember to blow gently, with a constant, smooth flow of air.

TOP TIP!
Why not record yourself so you can watch or listen back?

Now try these exercises. Remember to count through the long notes. The semibreves (whole notes) are worth four beats, so when we play them we have to count 1-2-3-4 in our head. The 'too' sound made with your tongue comes on number one. For the minims (half notes) we count 1-2, 1-2 again with a clear 'too' at the beginning of number one. Crotchets (quarter notes) are only one beat so we say a 'too' on every count: 1, 1, 1, 1 ... too-too-too-too!

Now take your middle finger and place it firmly over the second hole. Keep your thumb and first finger pressed down at the same time, just like you did for the B note. Covering holes lowers the pitch of the notes, so putting another finger down takes the pitch down one step. This two-finger note is an A. Try all of the rhythm exercises above on your new A finger positions, and listen carefully to the tone. Then alternate between a B and an A following the notes shown below:

Don't forget to keep counting through the long notes. So it becomes B-2-3-4, A-2-3-4 etc. for the semibreves (whole notes), and B-2, A-2 for the minims (half notes). How fast can you play the crotchets?

Keep your fingers near the holes even when you are not pressing them down, so you are always ready. The next note to learn is G. This is another step down in pitch, and we make a G by adding the next finger to the third hole on the front of the recorder. Try it now. Again, try the rhythm exercises on this new fingering.

As we cover the holes, there are fewer places for the air to get out, so it has to move further down the tube. If we blow too hard as we add fingers, the air splits inside the recorder and squeaks, so we have to blow more gently but firmly. Always check that you are making a nice sound.

Now you can play three notes, you are ready for some tunes! Practise them first by clapping, to make sure you have the right rhythm. Use the information in Chapter 1 to help you. One you're ready, play the whole tune, but just on a B note and following the rhythm, to practise your tonguing. Then try to play the notes by moving your fingers up and down to cover the holes.

TOP TIP!
Make sure when your fingers are pressed down they completely cover the hole on the recorder, forming a tight seal. If you don't, the air can escape out of the hole and you won't play the right note.

Hot Cross Buns

Hot cross buns!   Hot cross buns!

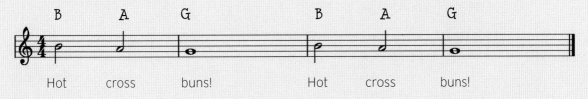

One a pen-ny two a pen-ny hot cross buns.

What do you notice about the first and second line of this tune?

Gently Sleep

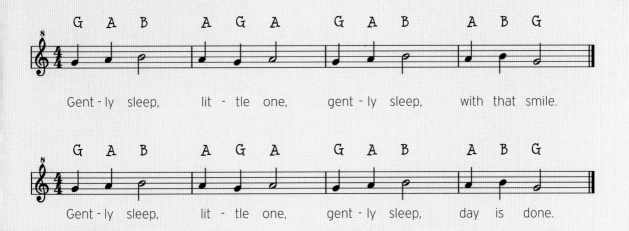

Gent-ly sleep, lit-tle one, gent-ly sleep, with that smile.

Gent-ly sleep, lit-tle one, gent-ly sleep, day is done.

Mary Had a Little Lamb

B A G A B B B | A A A | B D D

Ma - ry had a lit - tle lamb, lit - tle lamb lit - tle lamb

B A G A B B B B | A A B A G

Ma - ry had a lit - tle lamb, its fleece was white as snow.

Don't forget about your right hand! Rest the bottom half of the recorder on your right thumb and have your fingers hovering over the bottom four holes. Don't press them down, but have them ready for the next notes you will learn. Check your hands against the picture:

If you buy a **tutoring book** for the recorder, you will discover how to play lots more notes and find tunes to try. If you can play those, you should seriously consider getting a teacher!

Piano

The piano (or keyboard) is very easy to make a sound on: you just press the keys and notes happen! Try it now. However, if you want to play tunes, you need to know how to hold your hands and press the keys properly. You may have just been using your index fingers, but now you are going to use all ten fingers. To make it easier, we're going to give each finger a number. The thumb is 1, index finger (first finger) is 2, middle finger is 3, ring finger is 4 and little finger is 5. To that we will add an L for your left hand and R for your right hand.

You need to know how to find the notes. However big a piano or keyboard is, there is a repeated pattern of two black notes, a gap and then three black notes. Go to the middle of the pattern and find the white note to the immediate left of the first black note in the group of two. This is middle C, which we learnt about in Chapter 1.

Remember, middle C is the magic note where we cross over! It sits on its own little line BELOW me.

And it sits on the line ABOVE me!

Now let's find the correct position for your hands. Put your hands on your knees, keeping the fingers relaxed. Gently grip your kneecaps, like you would hold a cricket ball or baseball. Now, keeping that shape (and not dropping the imaginary ball), lift your hands up and put them on the keys in the following places:

Put your right thumb on middle C, then put each finger on the white notes going upwards.

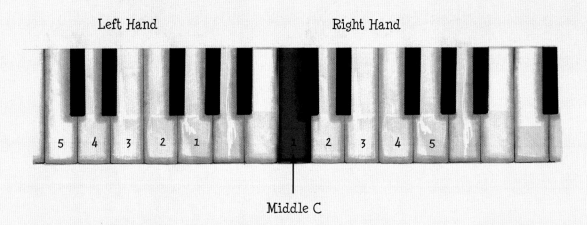

Place the little finger of your left hand on the C below middle C (check the picture to make sure you're doing it right), and then put a finger on every white note going upwards. Don't forget to imagine you've still got your half a baseball between your hands and the piano, and keep your wrists flat.

Experiment with playing one note at a time without moving your hands from these starting positions. Then try moving both hands from C to G at the same time. Now try both hands together, but going in opposite directions:

If you can do this and make your fingers move together at the exactly the same time, well done! We are ready to look at some tunes. Mostly, the higher notes played by the right hand form the tunes; the harmonies are formed by the low notes played by the left hand.

Try playing the melody using just the right-hand part, the top line. There are some quavers (eighth notes) in these tunes. We count them like this: 1-and-2-and-3-and-4-and. Then practise the left-hand part (bottom line) on its own; don't forget to count through the long notes. Then try them together. The notes line up where they need to sound together.

TOP TIP!
Why not get a friend to play one line, while you play the other? Then you could swap over.

Hot Cross Buns

Ode to Joy

On a piano we can also play chords. The easiest chord to play is the triad we learnt about in Chapter 1. Keeping your hands in the start position, just press down fingers 1, 3 and 5 at the same time. Again, practise this with one hand at a time and then both hands together. This is a C chord:

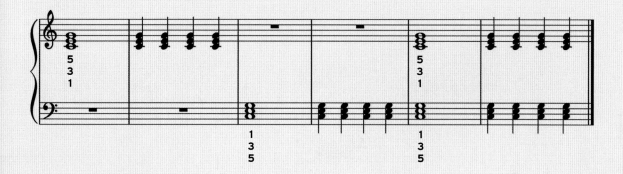

There are many more keys on the piano or keyboard than the ten we have been using so far! Starting on any note, we can make a triad by using fingers 1, 3 and 5, so we can make any chord we like. Keeping our fingers in the same position, we have to move them to the note we need to make the chord. The tune below uses C chords, F chords and G chords.

Also, if we want to play bigger tunes, we have to move our fingers off the starting position notes. This is where finger numbers become really useful. The tune on the next page uses a note outside our starting position. So, instead of playing a G note with finger 5, we stretch our hand and use finger 4. Then our little finger is ready to play the A note. Afterwards, we return to the starting hand position.

Twinkle, Twinkle, Little Star

Practise this tune for each hand separately at first. If the chords are too hard, try playing just the chord key note, as written under the music.

If this has taken your fancy, find a piano teacher near you or go to a class.

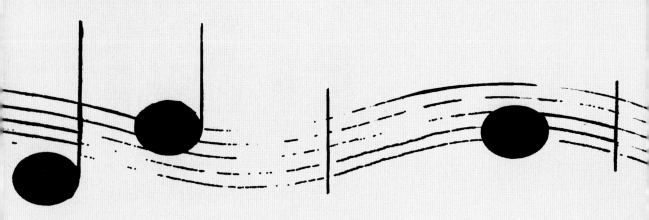

Guitar

Guitars are easy to make a sound on and are fantastic at accompanying other things, especially singing. When you have become good at playing, you could try singing and playing at the same time!

Start by holding the guitar with the strings facing away from you. Hug it into your belly and if it has a strap, put it over your shoulder. Sit down and tip the big bit on to your right knee, with the fretboard sticking up to the left. For now, you will only be using your right hand, so bring your elbow up and over the body of the guitar and put your fingers over the strings

where they sit over the hole (or **pickups**, if you are using an electric guitar). Hook your first finger over and practise plucking each string one by one. See if you can pluck gently to make a quiet sound, and then pluck harder to make a twanging sound.

Now try strumming. This is where you use the side of your thumb to stroke all the strings at once. Because all the strings are different notes, the sound will be a bit clashing, but see if you can make a funky rhythm by drawing your thumb over the strings over and over to the beat.

we will use these strings

Super! These are the two main ways of playing the guitar. We use plucking to play individual notes and make tunes, and strumming to play chords. We will be focusing on the top three strings of the guitar, which make the highest notes. These are G, B and E. In fact, these are the three strings that lie at the bottom as you are holding the guitar. See if you can strum these three on their own.

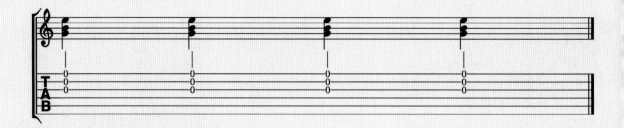

This makes an E chord.

Guitars have a middle to high sound, so use the treble clef or a special type of music just for guitars, which is called tablature, or **tab** for short. Tab has six lines for the stave, not five, and the lines represent the strings on the guitar rather than notes of the scale. Only the lines are used, not the spaces, and instead of blobs there are numbers. The numbers represent the finger you put down over that number of fret.

This is where your left hand comes in. Grip your thumb and fingers together loosely around the top end of the fretboard. Your thumb is resting on the back of the fretboard, your index finger (first finger) becomes finger 1, your middle finger is finger 2, and so on.

Each fret is one semitone, so to go from a G to an A you have to put down your second finger, but to go from a B to a C you put your first finger down. Practise the finger-hopping exercises below. The first one practises putting your finger down on the fret. The second one practises changing the finger at the same time as plucking the open E string at the top.

TOP TIP!
If your fingers are getting sore, you're probably doing it properly. The strings are metal and require a lot of finger strength to pluck them. Guitarists and all strings players build up extra hard skin on their fingers to compensate for all that plucking. With practice, you can too. Some guitarists use a little plastic disc called a plectrum to pluck the strings instead; you could try this too.

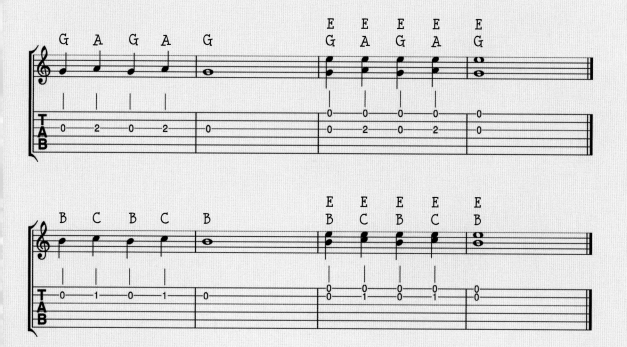

Now you are ready to try some tunes. We have looked at all of these tunes on the recorder and piano, so you should be familiar with them. Practise slowly and keep checking on your fingers to be sure they are going down in the right place. When you put a finger down, press the string against the horizontal metal fret strip. Your finger should be pressing between the fret you want and the last fret.

For the B, we are using our first finger and the first fret. This is the first metal strip from the top, or head of the guitar. Put your finger down in that gap, but press it right up against the metal so the string is held against the fret. For our A we need finger two and to count down to the second gap between the fret strips. Press your finger up to the next fret bar and so on, so we always press to the side that is closest to the body of the guitar. Check you are not squashing any of the other strings with the rest of your hand, especially when strumming or the wrong notes will come out! Remember the baseball grip we used to play the piano? Keep a space in the palm of your hand, even when pressing your fingers down, in the shape of a catcher's mitt.

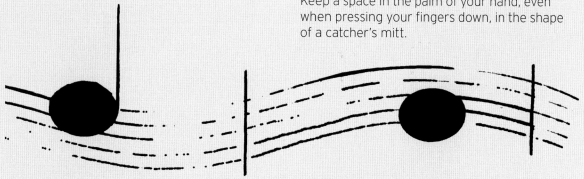

Hot Cross Buns

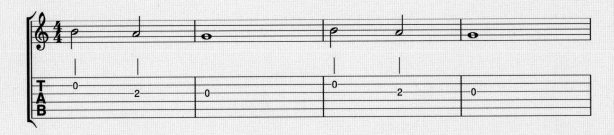

These tunes use an extra note that we have not yet looked at – D. D you will already know, is one step higher than our C and is therefore played on our B string (second from bottom) but this time with our third finger, on the third fret. Try playing the D on its own first, then try hopping between the C and D like we did in the warm up exercise. Can you go from B to C to D and back again by moving up the frets?.

Mary Had a Little Lamb

Twinkle, Twinkle, Little Star

There are many different styles and traditions in playing the guitar. If you can play the exercises above and want to try more, look at some tutorials online and then find a teacher or class that does the style you want to do.

Classical, Latin, jazz, rock, pop ... there are so many styles of music you can play on guitar.

And piano!

Yes, but they all have different traditions and ways of doing things.

I think it's time we found out more about them.

5
TYPES OF MUSIC

Now you know about many different types of instruments and may have had a go on some of them. But where can we hear these instruments being played by top musicians? It is just as important to listen to music as it is to make it. Listening to professionals gives you something to aspire to and reminds you how great an instrument can be, especially when you are finding practising it is tough. Also, you can learn lots from watching musicians. You don't just learn about the music and the instruments, but also how to act and perform as a musician in that style, as music has many different traditions.

If you like the violin, check out a symphony orchestra; if saxophone is your thing, look up a jazz band; and if you love the guitar, go to a rock gig and watch the awe-inspiring solos!

Classical

Classical music is a really broad **genre**, and a lot of people will say they don't like it when it is really only one tiny bit of classical music that they don't like. Have you ever seen any of the Star Wars films? They have great music in them and that is classical music!

Roughly speaking, classical music can be divided into periods of time, as the music has changed throughout history. Classical music is written down for the performers, using the **notation** we looked at in Chapter 1. It is usually written for traditional instruments and voices, though in modern times, composers have started to use electronics and technology to manipulate sounds. Each period of classical music had important composers. The main periods of classical music are:

Musical period	Mood and style	Instruments and ensembles	Main composers
Baroque 1600–1750	Simple melodies based on scales and arpeggios, but repeated a lot and layered to make complex textures. Dynamics were sudden and limited to forte (loud) and piano (quiet).	• Small, strings-based orchestras. • Operas – singers and orchestra tell a story in a staged show. • Harpsichords and organs instead of pianos.	• Claudio Monteverdi • Arcangelo Corelli • Johann Sebastian Bach • George F. Handel

Musical period	Mood and style	Instruments and ensembles	Main composers
Classical 1750–1830	Elegant, balanced and pretty melodies with strong harmonies and chords to accompany. Dynamics were limited but now included crescendos and diminuendos.	• Orchestras had more woodwind. • The clarinet and piano were invented! • String quartets became really popular, as well as other chamber groups including piano and woodwind.	• Wolfgang Amadeus Mozart • Joseph Haydn • Carl Stamitz • Luigi Boccherini
Romantic 1830–1900	Long, expressive melodies. Use of chromatic notes and chords to make more expressive harmonies. Big use of dynamics.	• Large orchestras with lots of brass and percussion. • Operas became long and dramatic. • Piano became a really popular solo instrument.	• Ludwig van Beethoven • Gioachino Rossini • Johannes Brahms • Pyotr Tchaikovsky • Edward Elgar
Twentieth century 1900–2000	Influenced by folk music and jazz music – simple melodies made complex, jazzy chords and unusual rhythms.	• Operas and musical theatre (popular music operas). • Brass chamber groups became more popular.	• Gustav Mahler • Claude Debussy • Richard Strauss • Ralph Vaughan Williams • Arnold Schoenberg
Contemporary 2000–today	Can be taken from a particular tradition or be a fusion of different styles. Lots of music written for TV, games etc., so this is led by the drama.	• Orchestras use electric instruments and jazz instruments such as the bass guitar and saxophone. • Many ensembles record and produce albums.	• Peter Maxwell Davies • Arvo Pärt • Howard Shore • Danny Elfman

You can hear classical music in all sorts of places. At concert halls, you can buy tickets to see a symphony or ballet or opera. These shows are often fancy and extravagant, with beautiful costumes and scenery. The musicians, dancers and singers all dress up in ball gowns and dinner jackets. People in the audience often like to dress up too, and have food and drinks before the show and in the interval. You sit quietly to take the music in and clap enthusiastically when the performers have finished and stand up at the front of the stage to take their bows.

More and more, however, orchestras and opera companies are taking the performances out of the concert hall and to the public. You might see a flash mob in a station or busking on the streets. Many of them do open days and workshops, where you can go and make music with the musicians during the day, before watching a performance. These are informal occasions, so you can wear your everyday clothes and have snack breaks!

Almost all films and television shows have some classical music in them. Sometimes, classical music is mixed with one of the types of music we're going to look at below. This is called fusion and it can make a really exciting soundtrack that uses voices and orchestra to make music that is especially relevant to the topic of the film.

Why don't you see if you can find an opera house or symphony that has a family day?

Jazz

Jazz music is now famous and loved all over the world, but it started in New Orleans, Louisiana, USA. Around the year 1900, people of lots of different cultures were mixing in the areas around the port and shipyards. Traditional Native American songs and South American Latin music fused with rhythms from African and gospel music from the African American community. It was a time when more people were learning to read and write, and soon these new musical ideas were written down using the notation we've been learning. This sort of music had not been written down before, and people started adding other elements of classical music and European traditions.

People played old military instruments and orchestral instruments, as well as instruments they found. This led to a **line-up** of a **rhythm section** of bass (double bass and later bass guitar), guitar, drums and piano; and a **horn section** of wind instruments including clarinet, saxophone, trumpet, trombone and vocals. Notice that the word 'horn' here doesn't mean an actual horn, but any instrument that plays the melodies and harmonies in the jazz music. These instruments became the basis for the

jazz band we learned about in Chapter 3, but in reality, people played with any combination of instruments they could find. As long as there is a rhythm player and someone to play the melody, anything goes!

Although the music was written down, a lot of it was still left to chance and the best musicians would **improvise** their own tunes. This means they would make up melodies on the spot, based on the chords and scales of the piece, to show how good they were at their instruments. They would play according to the mood of the moment. People would travel to see the best musicians play over and over again, as no two performances were quite the same and the music was very exciting.

Unlike classical performances, where you wait until the end to clap, people show their appreciation of a jazz soloist by clapping and cheering at the end of the solo, whilst the others are still playing. The jazz halls and clubs where this music is played are more relaxed than concert halls, too. People dress casually and often eat and drink during a performance.

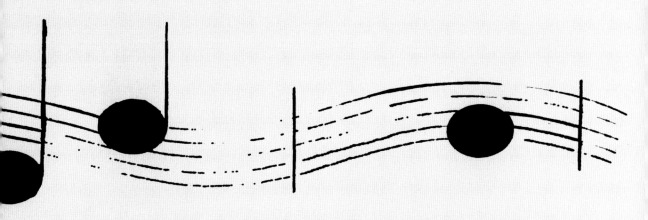

Pop and rock

Popular music, known as pop music, is everywhere: on the radio, on television, in shops and even in lifts! We can't get away from it, which is why it is the genre of music that most people are familiar with. Pop music is all about experimenting and selling as many records as possible!

Most pop music tries to be accessible - catchy and easy for you to sing and dance along to. However, a lot of artists try and get a message into their songs, usually about youth and culture, love, and even politics. They write about what is important to them and their fans. Pop music is mostly based on singing, and songs have a clear chorus and verses. Some types of pop music only use computer sounds and samples (bits of recorded noises and singing that are then manipulated with a computer) to make a track.

There are hundreds of different types of pop music, and some of these are:

𝄞 **Dance music** This has a really strong, driving beat, to get people moving! Often, there aren't many words but there are lots of catchy little tunes that are repeated and layered.

𝄞 **Rock music** This is loud and driven by guitars and heavy drums. The musicians mostly use live instruments (not computerized sounds) and lots of singing. Sometimes the singers scream and shout, and the music can sound quite angry.

Hip-hop music This type of music is often based around rapping and putting vocals over a given beat.

Pop music is much older than you probably think it is. It came about because of the invention of recording equipment and the increasing popularity of radio and later television. Some famous pop artists through time include:

Pop music is really easy to get hold of, as you can buy vinyl records or CDs, or download it online from iTunes, Apple Music and Spotify. However, a live performance is the most exciting way to listen to it, so go and see your favourite act on tour or go to a local music festival. Some people like to dress up like their favourite act, and either wear the same styles or wear their **merchandise**. Live pop gigs get very noisy and people scream and sing along: it is a lot of fun.

1940s	1950s	1960s	1970s	1980s	1990s	2000s
Frank Sinatra	Elvis Presley	The Beatles	ABBA	Michael Jackson	Britney Spears	Eminem

Who is your favourite pop artist of this decade? Try finding some interesting facts about him/her/them and their music.

Folk and world

Folk music is the music of a country's culture and tradition: whichever country you live in, it will have its own folk music. The term 'world music' is used to describe the folk music of countries other than our own. When we talk about folk music in Western Europe and the USA, we are referring to the tradition of music that wasn't written down, but each generation taught it to the next one. Examples of world music include:

Gamelan music A type of percussion music from Indonesia. Players use special metal xylophones and gongs as well as drums to help beat time. No one musician is more important than another - the important thing is playing together as an ensemble. It is highly respected and is used for special ceremonies. The music sounds mystical and twinkly.

Indian classical music This is based on special scales called ragas, which are passed down by ear from teacher to student. There are also set rhythm patterns called tal. There are different patterns for different moods, situations and time of day. Different regions and musical traditions use different instruments and mixes of patterns. All Indian classical music uses a lot of improvisation. The lead player will repeat the melody, or the rag, many times, but these get increasingly free and complex as he makes up his own patterns. Bollywood and bhangra music are a fusion of modern pop and classical styles, using the traditional instruments and scales.

Chinese music This uses scales of just five notes, which we call a pentatonic scale. The sound and timbre of the music is more important than the notes. Certain instruments and sounds are linked to different moods and even different seasons and elements, such as water. The music is often simple, with only one or two layers and long, flowing melodies that seem to have no start or finish.

African drumming and vocals This style uses a big range of traditional drums and percussion. The master drummer, who plays the most complex rhythms and solos, leads large groups of percussionists. He leads the sections by signalling to the group with a musical 'question', and then the group copies it back as an 'answer'. The music has lots of fast rhythms and beats and many layers of harmonies in the singing.

Samba and Latin American music A lot of the instruments we looked at in Chapter 2 are used here, and the music comes from the tradition of carnival. It is very cheerful and exciting music. There are often brass instruments to play fanfares, and many samba bands and groups march as part of the carnival procession. The many complex **cross-rhythms** encourage people to dance, and dances are named after them: the salsa, bossa nova, rhumba and merengue.

At folk gigs, people like to dance or tap along with their feet, and sing and hum the familiar melodies. In certain situations, people might grab an instrument and join in with the folk musicians! People dress casually or sometimes in their national costumes, or the costumes of the tradition of music that is being played.

Why not talk to your family about where they are from and the traditional music of that area? Look up artists who are still making that sort of music and listen to the sounds and ideas.

You could be listening to what your grandparents and great-grandparents listened to when they were young! Finding out about our heritage and culture helps us to know where we came from.

Yes, and music is such a big part of culture. It helps us to tell stories and discover our thoughts and feelings. We can also communicate with other people and share time together.

We hope you have enjoyed finding out about the weird and wonderful world of music with us.

Good luck on your musical journey!

Bye!

Glossary

4/4 time *See* Common time.

AA-BB structure A structure for a piece of music where there are two main tunes, which are repeated.

A-B structure A structure for a piece of music where there are two main tunes, first one known as the A idea, the second as the B idea.

A-B-A2 structure A structure for a piece of music where there are two main tunes. First the A tune is heard, then the B tune, then the A tune comes back again. Sometimes the A tune is changed a little bit, so it is known as A2.

Acoustic The name given to music that is produced without electricity or recording technology.

Amateur musician A musician who plays purely for fun and doesn't earn money from performances.

Amplifier Often just called an amp. An box that is plugged into mains electricity and electronic musical instruments, such as a guitar, and turns the electric signals from the instruments into proper audible sounds. Amplifiers also make the music sound louder, like when they are used with a microphone.

Arpeggio A broken chord. Instead of hearing all the notes of the chord sounded at once, we hear first the tonic note, then the third, then the fifth and finally the tonic, or key note again an octave higher.

Bar Units of regular patterns of beats that we divide music into. The length of the bar is decided by the time signature. Bars are divided up on the stave by bar lines.

Bar line The vertical line that runs through the stave, to divide up each bar.

Bassist A person who plays a bass guitar or double bass (often both).

Bassoonist A person who plays the bassoon.

Baton The stick (usually white) that a conductor uses to show the musicians the beats.

Beam The name we give to the horizontal lines that join together groups of quavers or semiquavers.

Beaters Sticks with different-sized bobbles on the end, which are used to play percussion instruments.

Beats The pulse of a piece of music, like a heartbeat. The beat is regular, either fast or slow, and rhythms fit into the beat.

Binary form Music that has a simple A-B structure, with two main tunes or ideas.

Bow A long, specially shaped stick, often made of wood, which is strung with horsehair. This is scraped over the strings of an instrument to make a sound.

Bowed strings Stringed instruments that are mostly played by scraping a bow across the strings. Some common bowed strings are the violin, viola, cello and double bass.

Bridge A section of a song that typically doesn't have any singing but links the other sections together. Often, it shows off the instruments or rhythm patterns of the song, to make a change from hearing the singer. It also gives the listener a chance to think about the words and tunes of the verse and chorus. A bridge is also the name for the wooden arch on a stringed instrument, such as a violin, that holds the strings up and away from the body of the instrument.

Cellist A person who plays the cello.

Chalumeau register The name given to the lowest notes of the clarinet, which sound more like a bassoon than the bright and clear high notes on the clarinet.

Chamber music Music played in small ensembles (fewer than ten musicians), where there is normally only one person per part of the music. The name comes from the eighteenth century, when it referred to the number of musicians who could fit comfortably into the king's chambers in the palaces of Europe.

Chord When a group of three or more notes is heard at the same time. The most common type of chord is the triad, built on the first, third and fifth notes of a key. Other notes can be added, or the order of notes can be changed, to alter the mood and sound.

Chorus This has two meanings. It can mean the main bit in a song, which is repeated several times with the main themes, words and tune. Or it can refer to a big choir, either on its own or as the backing singers to the soloists in an opera or a musical.

Chromatic When a tune or a chord uses notes from the chromatic scale that make clashing sounds.

Chromatic scale A scale that uses every note, including all the flats and sharps (both the black and white piano keys).

Clarinettist A person who plays the clarinet.

Clef The musical symbol that is placed at the top of the stave (at the beginning of the music and on every line afterwards), which shows the pitch of the music.

Colour When talking about music we mean the colour of the sound, so whether it is dark or sparkly. Another way of describing timbre.

Common time Another name for 4/4 time, which gets its name as because it is the most used time signature. Its symbol is a little curly C that goes in the place where the numbers usually go for the time signature.

Composer A person who thinks up musical ideas and creates music for other people to play. He or she will often write these down.

Concert pitch The agreed standard for tuning musical instruments. People who play in ensembles use it in order to play together.

Conductor The musician who stands before an ensemble and leads the players, telling them when and how to play by moving his or her hands or a stick called a baton. The conductor also leads the creative ideas in rehearsals.

Conservatoire A special university (college) for musicians, where they study their instruments and performance at a professional level.

Contrabassoon A giant bassoon that sounds one octave lower than a normal bassoon. It is a subsidiary instrument, so is played by a person who plays regular bassoon, too.

Conventional tuning Instruments that use conventional tuning are instruments that aren't transposing instruments. So when they play a C, it sounds exactly like the C on the piano.

Coordination The skill of using several parts of our bodies at once. For example we need coordination to play a drum kit as we have to use the pedals with our feet and sticks with our hands at precisely the right time as well as using our eyes and ears to read the music or watch the bandleader and listen to the group.

Cor anglais An instrument that uses a double reed; it is like an oboe but bigger and deeper, with a very mellow and beautiful sound.

Cornet An instrument like a trumpet but with a more mellow sound. Often played in military and brass bands.

Crescendo A term that means gradually getting louder.

Crook The part on a wind or brass instrument that attaches the mouthpiece or reed to the main bit of the instrument. Some instruments have a set of different-sized crooks that they can swap between.

Cross-rhythm The name given to a rhythm pattern that doesn't fit with the regular beat of the song and therefore doesn't sound quite in time with it. The strong beats come at odd places, not necessarily at the beginning of the bar.

Crotchet (quarter note) A note lasting one beat.

Damper pedal The right-hand pedal on a modern piano which, when pressed, makes the notes smooth into each other and resonate for longer.

Degrees of the scale The name we give to each step of a scale. In regular major or minor scales, there are seven steps before we repeat the starting note. Each step has a special name or can be referred to by number. For example, D is the second degree of the C major scale because it is the second note up.

Diminuendo Gradually getting quieter.

Distortion pedal An electronic device that can be controlled with the foot. It can be attached to an electronic instrument, usually a guitar, and used to alter the sound for special effect.

Dotted crotchet A note lasting one and a half beats.

Dotted minim A note lasting three beats.

Dotted quaver A note lasting three-quarters of a beat.

Dotted rhythm When we use a dotted note of any value paired with a single shorter note to round up the number of beats. Examples are: a dotted minim and a crotchet, a dotted crotchet and a quaver, a dotted quaver and a semiquaver.

Double bassist A person who plays the double bass. Often just called a bassist.

Double reed A reed made out of two separate pieces of wood tied together. It is placed directly into the lips to form the mouthpiece of the oboe and bassoon.

Drummer A person who plays the drums, usually a drum kit.

Duet Two musicians playing together, in two parts.

Dynamics The varying levels of volume used when performing a piece of music to make it more dramatic.

Elements of music The different features that make up music, which help us create it and understand it.

Embouchure The shape of a wind or brass player's lips as he or she squeezes the lip muscles to produce a sound on the instrument.

Ensemble A group of artists or musicians, such as an orchestra, band or dance troupe. This can be anything from a duet to a company of hundreds of people.

Fingerboard The long, flat, stick-like part of a stringed instrument on which the strings are pressed to make the changes of notes.

Fingering The pattern (e.g. the number of holes to cover or valves to press) to make a specific note, or order of fingers (e.g. which finger to press a key with on a piano) to make a tune.

Flat A type of note. It has a symbol that goes in front of a note to make it lower in pitch by half a step or a semitone.

Flautist A person who plays the flute.

Flugelhorn A small horn in B flat which is very similar to a trumpet and has a mellow sound.

Forte Loud.

Fortissimo Very loud.

Freelancer (freelance musician) A professional musician who doesn't have a regular full-time job with any one band or symphony orchestra. He or she may play in several bands, across several styles of music, and do other musical jobs such as teaching or producing.

Fret The horizontal metal bars on a fingerboard that show where the semitones are.

Fretboard The long arm that sticks out of a stringed instrument, where we place our fingers on the strings to change a note.

Fusion Music and ideas from two or more different genres and cultures that have been mixed together to make a new type of music.

Genre The name we give to describe the different types of music, e.g. jazz and classical are different genres.

Gig When a musician does a performance, such as a concert. Gig tends to refer to professional paid concerts, especially ones in informal settings, such as a jazz band playing in a bar or club.

Glissando The swooping noise that is made when an instrument such as a trombone or violin slides between notes of two different pitches slowly.

Guitarist A person who plays the guitar, acoustic or electric (often both).

Harmony The chords and accompaniment of a tune.

Harpist A person who plays the harp.

Held notes When a note is sounded for several beats or longer.

Home key The key a piece starts and finishes in or is based around.

Homophonic texture A texture where the layers of music mostly move at the same time, making blocks of sounds.

Horn section The name given to the brass and woodwind sections of a jazz or pop band.

Improvise When a musician improvises, he or she makes up tunes on the spot. This can be based on a certain set of chords or scales or a particular musical tradition.

Introduction The opening section of a piece of music, which introduces the key, style, mood and ideas before the main tunes or lyrics start.

Key The main scale that a piece is written in, which gives it its colour and mood. Each key has a different number of sharps and flats, which are shown at the beginning of the music by the key signature.

Keynote The note of the scale or key a piece is in. Also called the tonic.

Keys The round pads that sit over the holes on wind instruments, or the white and black blocks on keyboard instruments that you press down with your fingers to make different notes.

Key signature The number of sharps or flats in a piece that show which key we are in. It is written on the stave at the beginning of the music.

Large ensemble A big group of usually more than ten musicians who are making music together. Some examples are a symphony orchestra or a big band.

Leader The first violinist of an ensemble, who decides how all the violins are going to play and gives signals for the others to follow when playing. The leader often plays all the solos, too.

Ligature A small piece of metal or leather that wraps around the mouthpiece of a saxophone or clarinet and is tightened to hold the reed on.

Line-up The name we give to either the different types of instruments or different performers.

Major scale A scale that follows the pattern of step, step, half-step, step, step, half-step. These scales sound happy and complete.

Mallets Special beaters for percussion instruments.

Manuscript paper Paper that you can print out or buy to write on. Instead of having lines to write words on, it has lines of staves to write musical notes on.

Melody The tune of a piece and the way it moves up and down by step or by leap.

Merchandise Products or gifts such as t-shirts, stickers and mugs that musicians produce and sell to advertise their 'brand', e.g. the name of their band and make additional money at their performances.

Metronome (Maelzel's metronome) A machine that clicks with a certain number of beats per minute, which musicians use to set the correct time and count beats.

Mezzo forte Medium loud.

Mezzo piano Medium quiet.

Middle C The C note in the middle of the piano where the treble and bass clef cross over.

Minim (half note) A note lasting two beats.

Minor scale A scale that follows the pattern of step, half-step, step, step, half-step, step. These scales sound sad and incomplete.

Mouthpiece The top part of a wind or brass instrument, which is placed on or between the lips. This is where the initial sound is made either by a reed or block, or by the player's lips buzzing.

Movement A complete section of a larger piece of music, such as an orchestral symphony.

Notation Written down music.

Oboist A person who plays the oboe.

Octave A gap of eight notes, where the notes at the start and the end share the same letter name but one sounds low and the other is high, like the notes at the start and end of a scale.

Octave-transposing instrument An instrument that doesn't sound different to conventionally tuned instruments such as the piano, but is very high or low. So the music for an octave-transposing instrument is written an octave higher or lower in order to appear on the clef. Examples include the double bass, guitar, piccolo and some recorders.

Oompah band a band made up of wind and brass instruments playing traditional German folk music, with alternating 'oom' beats from the bass instruments.

Organist A person who plays the organ.

Pads Rubber, felt or leather bits that protect the moving parts of the keys or valves on a metal instrument such as a flute.

Percussionist A person who plays percussion. This includes drums and drum kit, as well as extra percussion, such as the tambourine or cymbals, and also pitched percussion, like the xylophone and timpani. Normally a percussionist will have one area that he or she will specialize in.

Pianissimo Very quiet.

Pianist A person who plays the piano.

Piano A large instrument with a keyboard. Its case contains strings that are hit with little hammers according to which key is pressed. There are two types of acoustic piano: upright and grand, which have the strings laid out in different ways. 'Piano' is also a word used in a piece of music to mean 'quiet'.

Piccolo A half-size flute that sounds very high and shrill; a subsidiary instrument for flute players.

Pickup An electromagnetic device that looks like a metal spot that sits under the strings of all electric string instruments. It picks up the vibrations of the player plucking or bowing the string and turns it into electric signals.

Piston valves Valves on a brass instrument which are cylinders that move up and down to change the pitch of a note.

Pitch How high or low a note or an instrument sounds.

Pizzicato A special technique used for stringed instruments, where the strings are plucked to make a twanging sound, rather than using the bow.

Positions The specific places a musician puts his or her hands and/or fingers to play certain notes.

Professional musician A musician who has studied to achieve an excellent standard on their instrument and makes a career earning money from their performances.

Quartet A group of four musicians, each playing an individual part.

Quaver (eighth note) A note lasting half a beat.

Quintet A group of five musicians, each playing an individual part.

Range The distance between the highest and lowest note of a piece or instrument.

Reed The wooden strip that goes on the top of reed instruments and is used to vibrate the air that the musician blows across it.

Relative major and minor A major

and minor key that share the same key signature (number of sharps or flats required to make the correct patterns).

Repiano cornet Repiano refers to the musicians who play the tunes and upper notes, but are not the soloists or leaders. Often refers to the repiano cornet, a specific part for the cornet players in a brass band but also used in other music, such as baroque.

Rhythm The pattern of beats in a piece.

Rhythm section The name given to the guitars, keys, bass, percussion and drums of a pop or jazz band.

Rotary valves Valves on a brass instrument, which are cylinders that move sideways to change the pitch of the notes.

Sample A sound that has been created digitally, or recorded from an instrument or life, which is altered on a computer to be used in new music.

Saxophonist A person who plays the saxophone.

Scale A pattern of notes that move by step in a given key or mood.

Semibreve (whole note) A note lasting four beats.

Semiquaver (sixteenth note) A note lasting a quarter of a beat.

Semitone The smallest gap between notes (e.g. between a white and black note on the piano). A half-step of a scale.

Sharp A type of note. A symbol goes in front of a note to make it higher in pitch by half a step or a semitone.

Sight-reading The skill of reading music and creating it immediately on your instrument.

Slide The moving part of a trombone that is used to change the notes.

Small ensemble A group of up to ten musicians playing together. This type of performance is often called chamber music.

Solo One musician playing or singing on their own.

Soundtrack Music written for a TV programme, film or video games.

Spike The metal stick that comes out of the endpin of the cello and double bass or attaches to the bottom of the bassoon, contrabassoon and some of the large clarinets. It is put on the floor to hold the instrument up to the height of the musician.

Stave The five horizontal lines that the music is written on.

Stem The vertical lines that stick up up from the 'blob' (head) of a note. All notes have these except semibreves and breves.

String quartet A group of four strings players, typically two violins, a viola and a cello.

Structure The shape of a piece of music and the way that all the main tunes and ideas are put together in different sections.

Strumming A technique used on a guitar or other stringed instruments, where the thumb is rubbed across all the strings to make chords.

Subsidiary instrument A musical instrument that is similar to a person's main musical instrument, which he or she will sometimes play in an ensemble when the music requires it. For example, a piccolo is a subsidiary instrument to a flute. The skill of playing these subsidiary instruments is called doubling.

Symphony A big piece of music for an orchestra, normally in four parts. The word may also form part of the name of a traditional orchestra, such as the Boston Symphony Orchestra.

Tab A type of notation specifically for guitars, that doesn't use the lines of the stave but uses 6 lines to represent the 6 strings of the guitar.

Tempo How fast or slow the music is.

Ternary form Music that has a simple A-B-A structure.

Texture The 'thickness' of the music: the layers of the music, how complex they are, and the way that they fit together.

Timbre The sound quality or tone of an instrument, or a particular mix of instruments.

Time signature The number and type of beats of a piece of music. It is shown by a number symbol at the beginning of the music.

Timpanist A person who plays the timpani drums.

Tonality The character of a piece, which is determined by whether it is based in a major key (happy mood), a minor key (sad mood) or no key at all (strange mood).

Tonic The first note of a scale or key. The technical name for the key note.

Transposing instrument An instrument that sounds to be at a different pitch to the piano when they both play a C note. Music for such instruments has to be written out in different keys, or the player has to change the notes in their head to match the other instruments.

Transposition When a piece of music is moved up or down to a different key or note.

Trio A group of three musicians playing together.

Trombonist A person who plays the trombone.

Trumpeter A person who plays the trumpet.

Tubist A person who plays the tuba. Sometimes used to describe people who play the other instruments in the tuba family too, such as the euphonium (tenor tuba) and the baritone (tenor) and tenor (alto) horns.

Tuner A machine that people can match the pitch of their notes to, to make sure they are in tune with each other.

Tutoring book A book specifically written for one instrument or music theory, explaining all the notes and showing you all the fingerings with exercises to practice and pieces to play.

Unison When every musician plays the same notes at the same time. A type of homophonic texture.

Unpitched percussion Percussion instruments that cannot play specific notes, and therefore cannot play tunes, e.g. bass drum.

Verse The middle sections of a song, which use the same tune or chords (or both), but often with different words each time.

Vibrato A technique where a musician or singer wobbles the pitch of the note, without changing the note, to make it more interesting and expressive.

Violinist A person who plays the violin.

Violist A person who plays the viola.

Answers

p.18 Word Music

1. AGE 2. BADE 3. BEAD

4. CABBAGE 5. ACE

p.30 Music Maths

1. 4 or o

2. 5 or o ♩

3. 3 or ♩.

4. 2 or ♩

5. 1 or ♩

6. 2 or ♩

7. 4 or o

8. 5 or o ♩

9. 3 or ♩.

10. ½ or ♪

11. 2 or ♩

12. 7 or o ♩

13. 3½ or ♩..

14. 2 or ♩

p.31 Add the Bar Lines

Index